About the Author

Born in former Rhodesia, the author spent almost fifty years in Southern Africa before immigrating to Perth, Western Australia in 1986 with his family.

He has a BA in Art Practices and Communications, a Masters in Visual Communications (Magna Cum Laude) and a Diploma of Architecture.

Work experience has been varied as a consultant in visual and design communications, as an industrial artist and designer and building designer (MSIAD: Rhodesia/UK; MSDSA: South Africa; MDIA: Australia; MBDA: Western Australia).

He also spent over twenty years' service in part-time military and police service, mainly in training and public relations, and several years in African affairs.

Ordering Information:

Quantity sales: special discounts are available on quantity purchases by corporations, associations, and others. For details, contact the publisher at the address below.

Upham-Hill, Christopher W.
Born of Fire: The Omen

ISBN 9781641820752 (Paperback)
ISBN 9781641820769 (Hardback)
ISBN 9781641820745 (E-Book)

The main category of the book — Short stories

www.austinmacauley.com/us

First Published (2018)
Austin Macauley Publishers LLC
40 Wall Street, 28th Floor
New York, NY 10005
USA

mail-usa@austinmacauley.com
+1 (646) 5125767

Christopher W. Upham-Hill

BORN OF FIRE
The Omen

The Third Millennium in Nova Afrika

AUSTIN MACAULEY PUBLISHERS™

LONDON * CAMBRIDGE * NEW YORK * SHARJAH

The Winds of Tyranny

A dark cumulus cloud hung on the horizon of the Engelibizo Plateau. The Sabiluto had seen similar manifestations before, when prevailing winds swept swarms of locusts from the North. But this one differed, it was more ominous and it did not billow or change shape – nor did it draw closer or move in any direction. It merely hung there peeking over the horizon. Villagers tendered numerous explanations but none with substance. Days passed and the behemoth continued to loom without change, charging the atmosphere with apprehension. No one could complete a task without snatching intermittent glances at the aberration.

In an early diurnal ritual, Villagers gathered in the central community and market building. Laughter and giggles punctuated the women's aimless prattle as they selected their requirements from the display of produce and supplies. The men who tended the fields and forest outside the trench also assembled in the market place to discuss preparations for the coming day, providing a chance to have an early meal, plucked from the array of victuals on display.

A few villages took time to study the strange cloud with light–hearted banter. Children scampered around in play. Two boys tried out new fighting sticks in an amicable joust, each exaggerating the pain as their opponent achieved a strike.

Their antics drew an audience of mothers and children. Haste was not an ingredient of the Sabiluto's idyllic lifestyle.

A man stood akimbo and pointed at the cloud billowing from the horizon. He tilted his head towards his colleague next to him and snorted.
I can almost see a face.

His colleague replied.
Yes, so can I – an angry face.

A young woman standing behind them touched her chin – trepid.
It's making me nervous.

The second man chuckled.
It looks like my mother-in-law.

The other man joshed.
Ha, ha – and mine.

Another woman standing with them, also looking at the menacing apparition, thought.
Men - they all talk the same drivel.

In yard next to the central market a small gathering of spectators encircled the two jousting boys.

A concerned mother cautioned them.
Be careful of your fingers, you boys.

Another mother commented with a smirk.
    My boy can be such a little show-off at times.

Another woman called at the boys.
    C'mon, you two can do better than that.

Encourage, one boy took a wild swing with his staff
and yelled at his opponent.
    Whack! Take that.

The other retorted as the miss–aimed effort whizzed
harmlessly passed his head.
    Wa, ya missed.

Men smiled in nostalgia at the boys' efforts, knowing
that they were imitating the lionized Royal Guard, the
heroic idols of the Sabiluto. The guardsmen captured
the imagination of all young boys and were the
fantasy quarries of young flirtatious nubile hearts. Girls
dreamed of handsome Guardsmen rescuing them from
aggressors, to be carried away in powerful arms to live
in a romantic haze forever after.

A young boy, standing close to his mother, stopped
and turned his head – a sound snatched at his acuity.
He cupped a podgy hand to his ear and tugged his
mother's skirt for attention, but she remained absorbed
in the performance of the two jousting boys, laughing at
their amplified contortions. She attempted to pick up her
son to pacify him, but he pulled away disgruntled at her
inattentiveness, and ran to the open gates.

The sound reached other ears – heads turned to
listen – someone sibilated loudly.
S h h h

A rumbling sound drummed in the distance. Most
Villagers looked at the disquieting cloud, but it showed
no sign of change. No flashes of lightning to suggest that
the rumbling could be thunder. Then the earth vibrated
underfoot.

Someone confirmed the obvious.
Shh! It's like a rumbling sound.

Another announced.
The ground is vibrating.

Concern rippled through them – then a shout. A man
ran through the entrance, pointing excitedly across
the bridge.

He ran back into the compound, panting out a
warning.
Buffalo, buffalo!.

No one comprehended any danger in buffalo.
They had a reputation of being unpredictable and
warranted some respect when encountered, but they
were not a threat.

A Hunter, perched on the rails of the fence screamed at
what he saw – a herd of buffalo,

stretching for a mile, maybe more, ahead of swirling dust, stampeded through the fields towards them.

He jumped to the ground, shouting.
To the bridge – get to the bridge.

Hunters and Villagers responded alike to the alarm. Men charged through the gates to the drawbridge. Once beyond the fence, the realization of the threat manifested.

Two hundred paces before them, a wall of frenzied, bulging–eyed beasts, streaming demented saliva from gasping mouths bore down at them. Hunters and villagers grabbed at any available grip on the drawbridge.

A Hunter urged loudly.
Pull – pull – pull!

The wave of charging beasts reached the bridge as the men heaved to pull back the cumbersome structure. The leading animals rushed upon them with eyes glazed in hypnotic intent. Heavy curved horns were lowered in glistening readiness to pierce and gore flesh.

Before the bridge pulled away from the opposite edge, one buffalo managed to scramble onto it. A Hunter fired an arrow into the animal's knee.

It stumbled as a man raced forward and plunged his spear through its side and into its heart.

The other beasts poured over the brink into the trench as the bridge pulled away. Their was no attempt to stop. The impetus and congestion of the animals at the rear pushed them forward.

They slipped, struggled to maintain balance and quailed as they tumbled onto one another. Layers of writhing animals rapidly filled the trench. The villagers could see that the trench would soon fill. There seemed no limit to the size of the herd.

Once inside the fence, the men closed the gates and jammed whatever poles were at hand against the frames as hunters scrambled to the top of the fence With their bows in readiness for the first animals to cross over.

From their vantage point they saw the spread of the herd disappearing into a wall of opaque dust that extended out of sight. It appeared that every buffalo on the entire plateau had massed into one gigantic charging throng.

The juggernaut trampled across the backs of the animals that filled the trench and lunged at the gates and fence. Yelling panic seized everyone. Woman snatched their children while men ran for weapons. Others dived into the doorways of their homes as some stood transfixed in disbelief.

The structure held in groaning tension under the load – then split. The Hunters rained volleys of arrows into the swirling mass below but despite their tenacity and accuracy, the effort proved futile. The fence buckled under the black churning wave of demented bovine and flaying curved horns. The sound of clanking horns, whaling beasts, shouting men and screaming woman whirled into a cacophonous matrix.

The men on the fence jumped from the crumbling fence and scrambled to join the other village men who resolutely stood in a defensive line with their spears and knives ready to face the onslaught. The women and children retreated to shelter in the work sheds behind the houses, hoping that the buildings would absorb the energy of the animals.

The buffalo burst into the central square. Men flung their weapons at the massive animals. Their first strikes were fatal, but no opportunity offered a repeat action. The beasts were upon them. Desperate cries of pain and fear drowned in the thunder of the assault as the defence line crushed underfoot.

The sturdy brick homes, proven adequate to the most lashing storms, crumpled and collapsed under the compact wall of mauling muscle. The workshed refuge subjected next. The herd swirled around inside the village enclosure, around and around, unabated, churning and pulverizing in frenetic unison. The settlement's curtilage crumbled in a swirling cloud of dust and detritus as the herd crushed the Sabiluto and their village.

Then gone, as swiftly as they had arrived, the buffalo raced to the next settlement, leaving a scene of groaning and spluttering carnage. Few survived. To compound the calamity, eldritch ten-foot high whirlwinds, with wavering humanistic features, danced among the dead and the dying in uninhibited glee, before sweeping away to follow the deranged animals. The whirlwinds performed like herdsmen, harrowing the buffalo into frenzied behavior.

Simultaneously, in a forest adjacent to the village, Hunter Tela maintained vigilance over a group of forest workers stacking logs. Stout ropes secured around the stacks prevented them rolling away. The heavy timbers presented a danger to the unwary. Families and children frequented the woodlands to play, and the log piles were a favourite for clambering over, hence the precaution.

Two men passed Tela, shouldering a trunk, while another two, on top of the pile, already seven–feet high, laid and fitted the logs in position. Tela heard an unfamiliar sound – not thunder. He recalled the unusual cloud formation on the horizon, but this sound appeared to emanate from the forest. He turned an ear towards the enigma.

The eldest woodsman, standing atop the pile, stopped to listen as well. He called down.
What's that strange noize, Tela?

Tela shook his head, unsure.

One woodsman shouted from the summit of the woodpile, and pointed an agitated finger into the gloomy trees.
Look, look

Tela squinted in the same direction. Through the avenues between the tress, he glimpsed movement, spreading across the entire width of the forest floor.

He yelled at the two men closest to him, carrying a log.

Run – run for the trees, climb as fast as you can.

One man asked as he rolled his end of the log off his shoulder.

What is it?

Still uncertain, Tela screamed for urgency.

Just run, dammit – run

They responded, dropped the log without hesitation and ran for the nearest tree. The men on the woodpile also reacted. One man slid down and joined the sprint for the trees. But his haste rolled a top log onto the older man's foot, trapping it.

It proved too heavy for him to move on his own. Tela peered into the advancing turmoil.

Then the image emerged.

Gnus, thousands of them, stampeding straight for them, snorting with their heads bowed thrusting their sigmate horns forward, ripping through the forest undergrowth, tearing bark and branches from trunks. All had demented bulging eyes with frothing saliva streaming from panting mouths.

Tela shouted at him at the man on the woodpile as he ran for the nearest tree.
Get off there.

The man responded in terror
My foot is caught.

Tela stopped and looked up at the trapped man. He assessed the predicament. Only seconds of opportunity availed. Escape for the woodsman was impossible.

Tela had been indoctrinated as a Hunter and, although barely into manhood. He had been the youngest man selected as a Hunter in the village's history. Now ensconsed in his role, he could not think of himself. His whole purpose in life directed him as a protector of his fellow villagers.

There would be no escape for Tela either. He would have to die helping the old man. Tela sprinted for the log pile and clambered up.

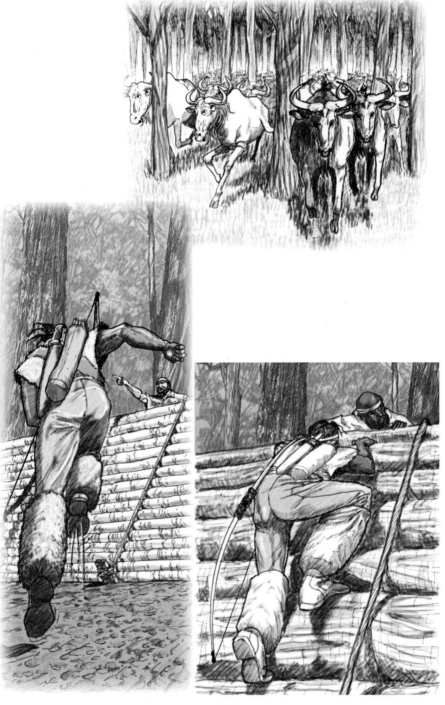

The old woodsman warned frantically.

Be careful, the woodpile is unsecured. If the animals knock it over we'll be crushed..

The herd pounded towards them. Tela reached him the moment the gnus burst through the trees.

Tela's mind raced as he sought an action.

Quick, roll logs towards them – they might stumble – it's our only chance.

Tela curled his strong arms under the log snaring the man's foot. With a coordinated heave, he the log rolled over the edge of the pile. It jounced against the logs beneath and jettisoned towards the herd, dislodging other logs as it progressed.

The leading animals arrived. Their spindly legs crashed into the spinning log and toppled over it as other logs bounced towards the herd. The following beasts crashed into the logs and stumbled. Those behind collided against the fallen ones to tumble into a contorting heap.

Tela and the woodsman sent another log down onto the pile of fallen animals. It dislodged more logs that rolled over the struggling animals and banged into more legs. The gnus fell to create a barrier too high for the charging beasts to jump, although some attempted to scramble over it but fell back.

Tela sprang to his feet and tugged the bow from his shoulder. In a single motion he loaded an arrow and

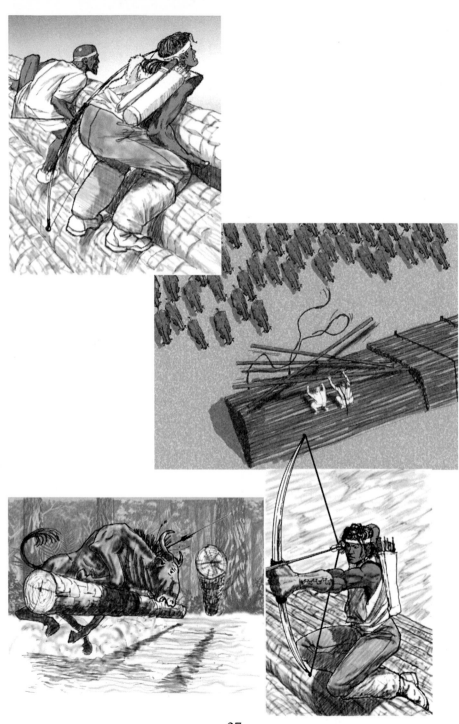

discharged it at the animals attempting to negotiate the pile of bodies and logs.

In seconds five gnus had fallen. The wall of fallen animals and logs grew into a wall, sufficient to veer the charging mass each side of the woodpile. The herd raced passed.

Then whirlwinds, with fierce indistinct faces, chased the animals with eerie screeches and hovered to threaten Tela and the woodsman. Then they were gone, leaving the men gasping in their residual dusty wake.

Tela called into the opaqueness to the other woodsmen, he had last seen hurtling towards the safety of the nearest trees.
Are you alright?

He heard the replies drift down from the canopy.
Yes. What the hell was that? I have never seen that before.

Echoes of, **Me, neither,** joined his confused question.

Tela and the older woodsman climbed down the end of the pile, not trusting the stability to descend down its sloping sides. He saw the other two men sliding down the trunk of a nearby tree.

Tela, satisfied that his duty to the woodsmen had been fulfilled, added,

The herd headed for the village. I'm going there now. I fear the worst.

He ran off into the dust.

The magnitude of the devastation stunned Tela. The whole area, including where his home had stood as a tranquil sanctuary, lay annihilated. But it was not the gnus that had caused the onslaught – it was buffalo.

Their bodies and those of villagers, some whole, others ripped apart, churned together with the shattered building debris. No house, shed or building, not even the market, stood complete. The fence lay flattened along most of the perimeter, its stout posts leaning in disarray.

Some wounded buffalo stood frozen or staggered around dazed. Animals at the top of the trenches struggled to dislodge their legs wedged between or punctured into the bodies below. Moans and bellows of pain and despair wafted eerily through the desolate dust that doused the carnage.

Tela shuffled into the dense miasma, compelling himself forward against the overwhelming reluctance at what he would discover. His mother and father, his beautiful lissome sister and his younger brother Gono were in there – somewhere. He stepped over body parts, severed

arms still clenched quarter swords, signifying final acts of bravery, open dead eyes starred at him from every direction.

His mind spun in emotional agitation.

Oh Mtombo, what a disaster - my family - my parents - my beautiful sister - my young brother, Gono - where are they - where are they? What is happening? Gnus stampeding in the forest - buffalo destroying our homes - what has made this happen? I cannot believe this devastation - all these buffalo. What sort of evil can inflict such carnage.

And those dust devils - such unreal creatures of sheer evil enraging animals and directing them. Who could posses such power?

He turned his face, distorted in anguish, to the sky and appealed..

How do I avenge this infamy – how can I...?

Tela then looked ahead. A hazy figure stood stiff, shoulders drooped and encrusted in monochromatic gore and dust. Only the eyes moved to look at Tela. Tela knew who he was – Gono.

33

Tela stepped towards his brother.
Gono.

Their eyes met.

Gono sibilated.
Tela.

He shook his head, a brief conclusive gesture – the others had perished. Tela embraced his sibling. He seemed bigger now. In the milieu of disaster, the boy had become a man.

He could think of little in the weight of his grief. His young brother stood motionless and expressionless, all feeling now concealed behind a layer emotional scar tissue.

Tela saw a fallen Hunter nearby. Did he know him? He could not tell as the man's face had been crushed in. He banished any attempt at recall.
Tela retrieved the man's paraphernalia. He sought a purposeful diversion against their overwhelming grief. Tela knelt before his brother and looped the crossed hide sashes over his shoulders.

They were from a zebra and supported a quiver of arrows and the scabbard for a quarter sword. He stood and handed Gono the sword attached to the shaft of a spear.

As a hunter, I have the authority to anoint another hunter into our league such as a retiring hunter once did for me. He bestowed his equipment onto me for he had no further use of it.

Tela gripped his brother's shoulders to confirm his actions.

Those who once owned these proud weapons, also have no further use of them. Now they are yours. Welcome to the Hunters, Gono, you are now dedicated to protect, guard and police the Sabiluto Villagers and the Baqala, the first people of the Engelibizo plateau. You are also required to bring fresh meat to your village each day. That is your duty.

Tela forced a smile.

One thing is for sure, Gono, you are definitely the youngest and smallest Hunter ever elected but you will grow, my brother, as will your skill. Come we have work to do.

Gono peered around his brother's large frame to see a wounded buffalo staggering towards them in a stiff and ungainly gait.

In a surge of anger, he rushed forward, almost knocking over Tela, who staggered back in surprize. Sprinting to the sluggish animal, Gono plunged the spear into the beast's side and through its heart.

Gono screamed.
Die you dog of the Devil.

The massive animal, managed a weak bellow as it
toppled over, kicking its legs in a final effort. Gono
extracts the bloody weapon and thrusts it down again
in spray of gore; and again; and again. Gono's eyes
were wide in rage as blood splattered across his face
and body.

Tela intervened and gripped his wrist.
*It's dead, Gono – preserve you rage for your
ultimate enemies. You will meet them aplenty – too
soon, I fear.*

It took some time before Gono's trembling yielded to
sobbing. Tela, crimping his eyes to control his own
lachrymation, held Gono in his arms and patted his
back. He could think of nothing else to do.

A cry of despair turned his attention to the four
forestry men who had followed him. One of them had
recognized a body – a relative – a friend?

Tela pulled back from his brother and wiped the
caked dirt from his young brother's face and gave a
weak smile. There was nothing to say.
In the dust–laden atmosphere, he could see the
murky figures of the forestry men moving about and
gesticulating their grief. Still gripping Gono around his
shoulders, he stepped into the centre of the imbroglio.

He waved an arm to attract their attention.
  Men, come over here, come here.

One man, grief stricken lay beside his trampled wife
and wailed. His colleague helped him to a stand and
dragged him away from the corpse.
 Tela knew he had to introduce a distraction before
they all submerged into the quicksand of despair. They
gathered around, hunched in trauma.

  Tela mustered as much resolution as he could.
    We must stay together. We must stay together to
    survive. Do not waste the efforts of the fallen by be-
    ing weak ourselves – that will betray their sacrifice.
    If we are not strong – we will also perish.

  One man interjected, his voice feeble in despair, as
he waved a hand around the scene.
    Survive for what? Where is my family – my friends –
    my home? What else is there?

  Tela reached out and grabbed his arm.
    Brother, we must be firm – we must.

Enervated, Tela felt his knees weaken and he sat
down, pulling his brother down next to him. The others
interpreted it as edification and sat down in front of
him, briefly deflecting attention from their grief.

One man wiped his eyes and muttered,
What do we do now?

Tela had no idea. His own bubble of remorse choked his
emotions and blocked reason. He knew that if it burst,
he would be unable to offer any guidance. He was,
after all, a Hunter. The village had elected him to this
post because he displayed leadership, equanimity and
skills, despite being only nineteen.

He had also dedicated his attention to the prospect of,
one day, presenting himself for selection to the Royal
Guard. In a condensation of time, all those challenges
had assembled before of him, questioning his probity.

Tela mustered his strength and croaked.
We must be strong — stronger than ever before.

He dabbed moisture from his nostrils with the back of
his hand and gave Gono a hug.
*We must not look upon the dead with horror or
despair. We must retrieve them from the debris
and bury them. All cannot be dead. There must be
survivors. Let us search for them, now — we must
begin now!*

*There is little time. The carrion and predators
will soon gather in multitudes, as soon as the air
clears. They will gorge on the buffalo for now, but
others will come — we will be their*

target. We must not leave our loved ones to be food
for them.

He stood and raized his face,
    Come brothers, let us start the task that destiny
    has thrust upon us. Let us do it with vigour and
    pride.

Tela swept his hand across the vista,
    There are still live buffalo around. Most are dazed
    and wounded, but they could be dangerous.

He indicated to the forestry men,
    You – you go and search for the fallen Sabiluto.
    Gono and I will protect you from the animals.

They heard voices behind them. Some people ran up to
them, five in all, explaining with agitation how they had
been in the fields when the stampede swept through. It
missed them by a few paces – they were the lucky ones.
And those minatory whirlwinds did not see them hiding
in corn

Not wishing to waste time on narratives, there would
    be plenty of time for that later, Tela asserted,
    We must search for survivors, quickly. Follow Gono
    and me and look out for buffalo. Not one more
    Sabiluto will fall to them – that, I swear.

He pointed into the fog with his bow.
  Let's go.

From the farrago of flesh and rubble, they heard groans
and moans. Tela and Gono stood sentry, while the
others launched themselves into the morass.

A buffalo limped passed. It died before it accomplished
another step. Gono, emulating his brother's toxophily,
thudded two arrows into the beast's neck. Tela grimaced
an expression of approval – his sibling really had
grown.

  As the villagers immersed themselves in cleaning
  and attending the victims Tela continued to instruct,
  **As soon as we can – we must burn all the bodies
  and carcasses, before disease takes over and the
  carrion arrive.**

The others had no alternative suggestions and obeyed
their young leader without hesitation.

By early afternoon, all surviving animals in the village
had been destroyed and hauled to the trench.

The gruesome undertaking of rummaging through the
building rubble in search of the remaining deceased took
them to dusk. Most of the accessible bodies had been
lowered into the trench and collocated with respect. Only
cries of anguish interjected the process, as they

recognized a loved– one. Tela and Gono had their own elegiac duty to perform.

Being a Hunter, Tela and his family occupied one of the houses adjacent to the entrance gates. They had been the first to succumb to the onslaught. His mother and sister had been inside preparing breakfast, unaware of the developing disaster.

Gono had been helping his father service the windmill. Gono had climbed to the deck below the blades where he witnessed the whole shocking event before it disappeared in an opaque cloud. He had seen his father race towards the surging animals, desperate to reach his wife and daughter – he did not last long.

The windmill buckled under Gono. He clung to it, as it slowly collapsed. By the time he landed, the herd had moved on. Only whirlwinds swirled around him. Stunned, he lay motionless for a while, before struggling to his feet and staggered to his home. He passed his father, crushed, almost beyond recognition. His house did not exist. Not even two bricks stood upright. Among the wreckage, he saw two hands in a clasp – one his mother's; the other his sister. Then, stiff with shock, he looked up and there stood Tela, effulgent and so strong – so alive.

Twenty of the villagers had survived. Some of them with broken bones and lacerations. Another ten were found alive, but with little hope. Twenty had perished outright. They lit torches to enable burial through the night, and hold the hands of the dying. Exhausted, one by one, the survivors collapsed to rest. But there would be no respite. The whirlwinds struck again an hour later.

The Royal Court settlement climbed in its five circular terraces from the high stone base above a surrounding conglomerate of separate smoky villages. The vista across the Engelibizo Plateau from the elevated terraces of the Royal Court spread unimpeded to a feint horizon.

The seasonal spectacle of migrating wild life crossing the enormous stage, had become a feature. Everyone, from the benevolent King Taba to apprentice cleaning maids gathered at convenient viewing points to witness the events. Repeated gesticulations and ovations rippled through the spectators. Tens of thousand bovine, antelope, zebra and plodding, trumpeting elephant, swarmed around the containment of villages at the base of the Royal Court as they flowed passed for days to their new pastures.

The farmers knew the routine and allowed their fields to remain fallow until the migratory season ended before replanting. They took advantage of the mobile refertilization process and turned the soil soon after the herds had passed.

The sighting of an unusually large herd of elephant, heading in the direction of the royal settlement, brought a flurry of attention, especially when they noticed the vigorous pace of the animals and the manner in which they crammed onto the axial highway.

Alarm rattled through the spectators when the herd appeared to completely trample through a village close to the highway. The made no attempt to veer around and it just washed over it in an animalistic avalanche, filling the external trenches with their own bodies. Whirlwinds appeared to be chasing the heard, emanating a strange caterwaul.

Angst mounted further when someone on the higher terrace uttered loudly.
They're coming straight for us.

King Taba, standing at the edge of the throne terrace to view the herd, grasped at the anomally.
I don"t believe it. They're charging the Royal Court.

Councillor Potonoka, at his side added,
My God, there must be thousands of them – what the hell is this?

Instinct generated his first command. He yelled down the approach slope to the guards on the lower terrace.
Pull the bridge back, now.

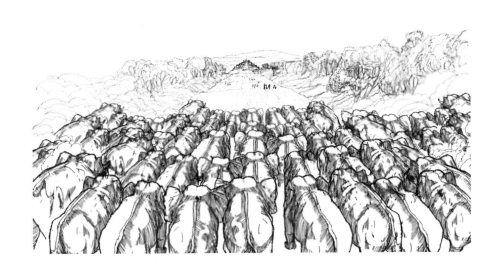

The elephant approached at a trot, gathering pace and were already only few hundred paces from the retractable bridge. The aggravation of the bizarre whirlwinds harassed their advance.

Potonoka screamed to energize the bewildered guards.
Move, move.

They could not see the problem from lower down.

Obediently, the guards rushed to the bridge, but too late, elephants had clambered onto it. Their weight had rendered sliding the bulky contraption impossible. Guards raced to attack.

Armed only with spears, they attempted to slam their blades into the knees of the lumbering giants while avoiding their flaying trunks swiping tusks. A whirlwind raced passed the elephant and swirled its anfractuous tail among the guards, sending them sprawling. Their bodies splattered underfoot as the surging beasts funnelled onto to the approach slope and trundled onto the lower terrace.

Trunks tossed people aside with the ease of bothersome debris. Others curled victims over the heads in their trunks and smashed them against their backs. Men, women and children were treated with equal disdain. Tusks sliced through abdomens, spraying out entrails while enormous flat feet crushed limbs, bodies and skulls.

Attempts to halt the assault had no effect. Beasts and humans tumbled over the edge of the lower terrace as the animals surged into the complex. Buildings distorted and collapsed as trees fell under the momentum. Then they reached the second terrace, repeating the demolition. Screams, yells, cries, and trumpeting stirred in a rising fog of horror.

Otasa noticed that some elephant, attempting to climb higher, floundered on the dew–damp lawn grass each side of the sloping central paved approach path. Whirlwinds that attempted to traverse the wet paving suddenly collapsed into muddy middens.

In a flash of inspiration, Otasa rushed down to some men on the next terrace, waiting in defence. Six large water tanks perched on high stands and located on the fourth and fifth terraces, delivered the settlement's water supply. They would be full at this time of the day. The windmill pumps would have worked through the night. Large controlling earthenware pipes drained the water to the complex's articulated channels.

Otasa shouted his instructions to the men,
Look, the elephant are slipping – the whirlwinds perish on the wet – break the pipes on the water tanks – quickly.

The men responded as women detached from their entranced terror to help. They scrambled

52

apelike up the water tower bracing. Standing each side of the outlets pipes, they beat them with an assortment of instruments. One by one the pipes cracked and sprayed out a fan of water, before spewing out their contents in thick columns.

Moments later, the water, contained in the narrow spaces between the row houses, gushed in a tidal wave towards the approach slope and the floundering elephant.

People scrambled onto roofs as the terraces filled. Water erupted from both sides of the approach slope. The lumbering elephant, already struggling with the slippery surface, lost all remaining traction. Falling onto knees and haunches to maintain balance. The animals slithered back in an exponential mass, carrying the remnants of the evil dust devils with them. A minutiae of advantage turned towards the Sabiluto.

Someone shouted.
Add fire to the water.

It was a well known that elephant reacted with phobic panic towards fire – even small non–threatening ones, evoked odd behaviour. From the debris, the Sabiluto plucked any combustible material they could locate – roofing timber, furniture, doors, clothing – and set them alight. Using their spears the men flung the burning matter onto the animals on the lower terraces.

55

Pandemonium ensued. Smouldering beasts bolted
for the lower levels, scrambled, slipping and sliding,
through the ruined buildings and thudding into the
elephant crowding the bottom terrace. The impetus
carried the animals over the brink of the base wall and
onto the ground below.

The sight of burning and injured elephant falling,
trumpeting, over the edge, defused the ardour of the
remaining herd still milling around the perimeter wall
and the entrance bridge. Discouraged, they turned
and cantered away into the surrounding terrain,
interspersed with the demonic whirlwinds, lashing
them with their tails.

A cheer rose from the embattled settlement – they had
survived.

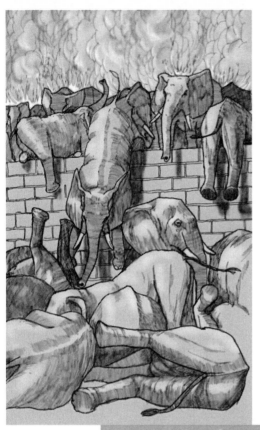

Further away a large man strode proudly along a path in front of his young bride. He had served his time in the Royal Guard, and now he had reached an age of retirement, usually his fortieth birthday. The men had the option to retire sooner, if they so desired, but the more senior men, stayed the full term.

According to the custom, while they served, the guardsmen practiced celibacy. Their choice as husbands dominated the list of ambitions that most eligible young women fostered. They waited in line for the moment when they could present their credentials as loyal loving partners to the next available guardsman. His personal attributes held little significance, being a guardsman, the ultimate criteria.

The path approached a thicket. Instinctively, the man brought his spear to the ready as the route ahead dissolve into the umbrous foliation. His senses hightened as they entered. He stopped to allow his wife to catch up. When she was close behind, he proceeded.

They launched themselves simultaneously – dark green ophidian tubes of tensile rage, six–foot long and as thick as an arm. Curved white fangs dripped deadly yellow venom. From the ground, from above, the giant reptiles clamped their jaws into every portion of exposed flesh. The guardsman slashed wildly at the overwhelming assault, hacking bodies in half.

Severed heads, latched into his flesh continued to inject their fatal potion. He bellowed in pain – his wife screamed – he could hardly distinguish her under writhing carpet of demented serpents. His adroitness with his weapons was ineffective against the number and ferocity of the serpents. More and more of them sprang from the thicket, twenty, thirty, more.

The weight of the snakes twisting around his body forced him to his knees. He could no longer hear his wife. They entwined his limbs in a writhing convoluted mass, pumping venom into his brain. Only a loud singing shrieked through his acumen, as life abated under the bombardment of chemical paralysis.

That evening the black cloud unleashed its intent. With typhonic savagery it discharged a funnel of wind across the countryside. Sweeping from side to side, it permeated a carpet of swirling dust devils.

As they sashayed across the plains, they gathered dust, earth and debris to increment their size and ferocity, reaching twenty feet and more in height. Nothing in their path withstood their onslaught as they rampaged mercilessly across the Engelebizo; at times travelling in extended lines for maximum effect, churning victims into gory spray in their grinding viscera.

Trees, huts, fences animals and humanity were also blasted away, to crash in pulverized disarray against any obstacle still sturdy enough to stand. With little respite, the devastating force of the meandering and whipping spouts ravaged the plains for the next two days. It seemed that nothing could survive – then they stopped.

A traumatized hush clasped the shattered landscape. Survivors, dirty, battered, quivering, and aghast at the destruction confronting them, sifted through the rubble, moaning in grief and disbelief. The atmosphere glowed in an ochre haze, saturated with particles that once represented the vibrant life of the plains.

The substance that had been the strength of the Sabiluto, their innate resistance to the iniquitous forces of nature, had been shattered. Was this to be their end? And, as the carrion gorged on the dead, the demonic whirlwinds returned to gleefully supervised the lurid spectacle.

The volume of reports reaching the Royal Court distressed the old benevolent King Taba. He and his entourage inspected the plains to review the aftermath of the savagery that had deracinated the lush surrounds to a dust bowl. Twelve burly men with shoulder straps fixed to bearers guided the royal litter. The bearers supported a deck on which the king sat in a padded chair. An arched canopy covered in skins shaded the deck.

A central axle and two large spoked wheels supported the trundling structure.

A headdress of shimmering white fur distinguished the king, and a single gold ear–ring dangled from his right ear lobe. He held the royal staff. A tuft of white crinkly hair quivered on his chin when he spoke. Twenty councillors, with shaven heads and dressed in white singlets that reached their ankles, preceded the litter.

Like the king, they wore the single gold ear–ring and carried their staffs, long polished wooden shafts, each culminating in a trumpet–shaped boss. Handmaidens and attendants followed the litter. A company of the Royal Guard flanked the litter comprising of fifty men in two staggered files on each side.

Having witnessed the results that water had on the whirlwinds, the Guards engage water as a weapon. Before proceeding on their inspection, bladders containing several gallons of water were prepared with shoulder straps to enable portage and a tube extending from the bottom and folded at the end allowed the water to be sprayed when the end fold was released. Suspended from the shoulder and held under the arm the bladder could be squeezed to discharge the water in a forceful jet.

When the royal procession stopped and lowered the front of the litter, handmaidens and councillors

climbed the ramp onto the deck to attend to their sovereign and hold a temporary court. Everywhere they travelled they witnessed the preternatural whirlwinds frolicking across the macabre stage, often rushing up to the royal party through the atmospheric fog, tantalising the guardsmen, prancing around them and withdrawing as if an unseen force reined them.

Never before had the Sabiluto encountered such apparitions. They had no doubt that a duende had invaded their land. Some of the whirlwinds barricaded the highways, reaching above the party, threatening while other whirlwinds closed in on the flanks and the rear to encircle them, forcing them to halt. The surrounding wall of screeching dust compressed into huge single disturbance, swirling over the royal party. It began close its base to create a funnel with the intent to suck the entire procession into its midst.

A single command activated the Guards. Instantaneously, they sprayed jets of water into the void above. As the liquid spread into the resonating funnel walls of the gathering cyclone, clouds of mud started to fall. They persisted with the water spray. In a few moments the giant feature collapsed in final lingering scream, leaving the gleaming white royal gathering dripping in wet mud.

With the horror satiating his mind, King Taba returned to the Royal Court, one of few structures

the holocaust spared. Nothing, he nor any councillor had ever seen before related to the occurrences they witnessed – nor could anyone recall their elders recounting anything similar. The court decided that they needed all the help they could get. And, if it was the supernatural confronting them, then it was to the supernatural they had to turn.

In the council chambers of the thatched Royal Court, Taba slumped enervated in his chair. The sullen demeanour of the councillors, seated on benches diagonally facing the king, reflected the foreboding. The pervading stench of the cremation fires, purging the carcasses of the elephant around the Place of the Throne exacerbated the mood.

While leaning with his cheek in his hand. King Taba uttered melancholy.

Otasa – Potonoka, what kind of evil strikes at us with such ferocity? What manner of power drives the wild life to attack in this way? And who can create whirlwinds to obey orders – at least, that's what it looks like. Someone is driving these creatures.

We have lived for centuries in relative understanding with our surroundings and the beasts of nature. Never has anything of this magnitude happened before.

69

Otasa, nearest to Taba, spoke – his voice rough with emotion.

My king, I do not think any of us doubt that we must seek the guidance of the Baqala diviners. Even if only to offer a suggestion, would be more than we can muster at this time. It is time for us to ask their diviners to show us some sign.

Potonoka, a constant companion to his older brother, responded.

No doubt, my king, the great cloud that hangs over the Engelibizo plateau harbours an evil spirit beyond our comprehension. We can only combat it with a greater supernatural power. But we do not have supernatural powers.

There is no one I know, not even the Royal Diviner Bakati, have such abilities – no one that I know of. We have always been pragmatic people, feigning any inducements towards spiritual beliefs. The Villagers are like that as well.

That leaves only the Baqala who have herbalists and soothsayers. Call them diviners if you wish, but they do not demonstrate any special prowess beyond the quotidian functions of our nation.

Otasa tapped his chin with a forefinger in thought before expanding on his brother's comments.

Perhaps, collectively they could muster some power of that nature. If through their individual levels of metaphysical manipulation are not enough then together in one place at one time they might achieve something in that direction – the whole being greater than the sum of the parts.

His proposition aroused interest in the council chamber. Slouching councillors straightened in intrigue.

Potonoka added a defuse.

To reach every diviner in the land would take months – to receive their findings would take even longer. Yet, if we are seeking their advice, can we afford to exclude any one of them? Anyone of them could harbour the answer.

Taba tugged his beard. The rest ruminated with their thoughts.

Bakati, the royal diviner, a devious and emaciated man with an abnormally bulbous stomach and reeked of strange herbal odours, had inveigled his way into the favour of the king, as many believed, with fallacies.

The moment of truth had arrived for him. Instantly, Bakati realized that, to retain the respect of the court, he should be the only one to manage the spiritual events of the nation – that was his job, not that of the councillors. He was not only the spiritual link of the Sabiluto of whom most were secular but the only respected authority to deal with the Baqala shamans.

Underlying his aggrandized position lurked his ambition to have his family enthroned one day. His sons and daughters stood so close to the royal prodigy that the chance of a union prevailed. King Taba was equally aware of the situation. The lineage of the throne had never verged this close to the threat of a non–royal inclusion.

Now, in this crisis, the opportunity to grab an advantage surfaced. Although everyone respected Bakati's role, he stood apart by choice, aloof. A definite repellent aura surrounded him and it was not just the odour of herbs, his attitude was recalcitrant. In discord with the rest of the Royal Court, he wore a skirt of multiple–coloured hide strands and shoulder bands of soft hide that crossed his chest. They announced his profession, as did the circle of guinea fowl feathers that made up his headdress. His red malaria stained eyes burned menacingly. He only carried a short fly swish, indicating that he had no need for weapons or maces – his power was sufficient.

Bakati rose from his seat at the far end of one bench and sauntered into the centre of the room, haughtily flicking his swish at imaginary flies, to face the king.

Why do you bother with the Baqala diviners? I am Baqala, as you are. We have all the capabilities that they have, we just choose not use them because of our hereditary appointments to the Sabiluto court.

King Taba, I will supervise this event. I alone will find a solution. If anyone has the insight to handle the Baqala diviners it is me. That is, if I consider such a move necessary, which at the moment, I do not. I have cast my solicitousness to the spirit world – the response indicates that this aberrance will move on.

I have made a number of consultations with my tokens, but there is no specific direction. Perhaps, a reshuffle of authority, your majesty, might bring a result.

Perhaps, I should head the councillors in this deliberation. With that authority, only subject to your intervention, perhaps, I could…

King Taba retorted loudly in an unusual outburst. Bakati, stop with your nonsense! This is not the time to introduce your ambitions.

The two men glared at each other intently. Taba leaned forward with a pronounced scowl.

If you insist on this pursuit, I will bar you from this debate and have you removed to your quarters . Do you understand.

Bakati grunted, flicked his swish with arrogance, ignoring the threat. He knew that the situation held greater significance than mere words, even those emanating from the throne.

He hissed.

So be it – but you would be better advised, at least until this threat is resolved, if you consult with me alone on this issue, before speaking to these spiritually depleted councillors.

He waved his switch around the chamber.

Taba continued to glare at him.

Do you never desist with your ambition, Bakati? This is not the time, nor the place to entertain your trifles.

Angrily Taba continued.

You place you own desires before the Sabiluto. You are a disgrace.

He concluded with an emphatic slap of his hand on the armrest and yelled towards the assembly area where the duty guards patrolled.

Guards.

Two burly figures filled the entrance to the chamber.
Take Bakati away! Confine him to his quarters until I
tell you otherwise.

The two guards gripped Bakati's upper arms. He tried to
shrug them away, but to no avail. They turned him and
walked out of the chamber to the open terrace.

Bakati glowered at Taba as he passed.

He mused.
*There is one thing I have learned, my
old time-expired king and that is that
your days have ended. There is a new
ruler on the way. I will serve him.*

Taba only felt it secure to continue once Bakati had left
the chamber, descended the terraces below the throne
house and halfway across the assembly area.

He turned to his councillors.
Send messengers immediately, and use every means
possible to instruct that every diviner, every single
one of them, that they must deliver some direction
by the end of this month.

They must forsake all other duties and concentrate
solely on this task – this is a royal command.

We will even include that useless charlatan Bakati when it suites the time.

Potonoka rose, always the paradigmatic councillor, and in his characteristic composure he spoke with resolution.

If reaching the shamans is time consuming, and that cannot be avoided, we could save much by calling them all to this place. They can deliberate en route. Here, we will hold a congress of Baqala shamans.

Collectively they can perform their incantations and ceremonies, draw from each other – encourage each other. Then, if an answer is found it will be available to use immediately. There may even be a lesson for Bakati – who knows.

The sarcasm prompted a relieving cachinnation. The court accepted his suggestion with a salutation. Now the moment of reciprocity had bloomed. No one knew for certain the depth of the Baqala's spiritual powers. Nothing of this magnitude had happened before to challenge their ability to this extent. Yet, to a man, the court acceded that the Sabiluto had no option. The combined and simultaneous incantations may just identify the perpetrator.

Another special group among the Sabiluto were the Messengers. Each village retained at least two Messengers. The selection of these men began at an early age, usually before their tenth birthday. Their sustained long–distance running ability stood as the their principal selection measure. They undertook extensive training, until on their sixteenth birthday they were initiated with their first solo despatch into the ranks of the Messengers.

The Messengers were the only Sabilito to have retained the skill of ciphering, in which they spent many hours of practice. It was not surprising that most of the soothsayers emanated from the Messengers when the arduous physical demand become difficult at an older age.

Inscribing charcoal onto a bleached cloth scroll and then sealing it with beeswax endured as their method of recording instructions to avoid inconsistencies. Once a Messenger received his instruction, he rapidly inscribed his scroll and rolled it around the shaft of a lightweight spear, covering it in a protective leather sleeve. They wrapped a thong, plaited around the spear's shaft, around their hand and gripped the spear. This represented the baton that each messenger passed to the next at the end of his prescribed route.

The new Messengers read the contents of the scrolls at the first opportunity, in case some misfortune beset the baton. The Messenger would then still be able to deliver the message to the next recipient who would immediately prepare a replacement. Memory training constituted a strong ingredient of their attributes. The Messengers, under instruction from the Baqala, learned the idiosyncrasies of the natural world to a corresponding level as the Hunters. Personal concealment and the dispensation of herbs that created scent distractions, during their frequent confrontations with predators, prioritized as an essential skill.

The Messengers conveyed the directive from the Royal Court to every corner of the plains, calling to the Place of the Throne a meeting of every diviner and prophet in the land. Drummers cast their rataplan signal through the anxious ochre miasma to precede the runners, racing to the scattered Baqala villages They passed a plenitude of disinterested gorged predators, which, a few days earlier, would have attacked with absolute aggression.

As the call permeated through the plateau, it aroused Shamans of every description, eager to participate in the resolution to defend the Engelibizo from the deleterious threat that faced them. It also roused some characters, that up to this point in time, many had considered metaphysical while others were known of but never seen; the Vatope people from the swamplands an example. Some travelled to the assembly in gregarious groups as others walked alone; Hosiyosiku, Queen of the Night, was one such personage.

Many had spoken of her existence, but few could recall actually seeing her. Sparse rumours and speculation circulated about her. The anomaly surrounding her existence exulted her legend. Some thought they saw her in the distance, or atop a rise, sashaying eerily to the Place of the Throne in billowing robes of long white feathers. But they were never definite, perhaps merely experiencing illusions in the murky air.

The assortment of diviners gathered on the forecourt and approach slopes to listen to their king. Sitting stiffly on his throne and firmly grasping his staff of office, as if for divine guidance,
Taba surveyed the assembly with gloomy eyes. Councillors stood nearby with Potonoka and Otasa on each side of the throne. The Royal Guard, in their green cloaks, red headband and armed with spears, stood equidistant around the lower platform and base of the structure.

Once the gathering had reached capacity, the king addressed them.
People of Engelibizo, the evil that has befallen our land has compelled me to bring you here. We, of this court, have concluded that to use your combined powers in one place, at one time, will expose this evil.

We do not believe that the same result can be accomplished with isolated and individual efforts.

84

85

We understand the abnormality of such a demand, but feel that the circumstances warrant the action. Many of you here have never met you piers, which makes this gathering even more unique. There are those of you who exist in legend alone, never having revealed yourselves before – another remarkable fact of this day.

Once the evil is revealed we can deal with it, but concealed, it can strike without warning. Each of you must perform your most magical rituals simultaneously to concentrate your powers. You must commence immediately and report you revelations to me without delay.

He paused and stretched his hands outwards.
Go now and do this.

Bakati stepped from the front of the crowd towards the base of the platform. Not wishing to be banished again he displayed acquiescences and spoke in a humble tone.
Mighty king of kings, the enormity of this objective suggests that novices should not tamper with it. Once again, I suggest that I, Bakati, take the responsibility for making contact with our tormentor. Let me, Bakati, diviner to the Royal Court, alone reveal the truth.

He paused and scanned the gathering behind him.
Let me burden the consequences alone.

Taba replied, steadfast, not wishing to stimulate
another incident.
Bakati, we need all our powers, including that of
novices, There is no doubt that without your contribution we would be that much weaker. Be the first,
by all means, to make known this enemy and your
status in this court will be confirmed, but if you are
not able to find the way and another does, there will
be no judgement passed or erosion of your place.
This is not a competition – this is survival. That will
be all on this matter.

Bakati, seeing his advantage slipping, continued.
Your majesty, I insist that the process be conduct-
ed under my authority...

Taba's attitude roughened. He thumped the arm of
the throne with his fist and his jaw flexed with anger.
Bakati, I have warned you already – this is not the
time to pursue your ambitions. If you continue to
place yourself ahead of the Sabiluto then I will have
you arrested permanently.

He leant forward to emphasize his warning.
   Do you understand me?

Bakati's eyes narrowed. He knew better than to challenge Taba at that time.

He bowed his head.
   Your majesty.

In dudgeon, he stepped back into the gathering, turned and left the arena.

The Search for Chetemoto

As twilight drew the curtain of night around the Place of the Throne, preparations mounted for the oncoming events. The small Vatope people, the inhabitants of the inhospitable swamplands, lit torches and squatted in a circle, concealed beneath cloaks and hoods made from the giant green swamp lizards; the same material as the cloaks of the Royal Guard. The cloaks draped over a stick along the top of their heads and plaited into their hair.

They launched into a slow rhythmic chant, hardly audible at first, slowly rising in intensity. Two of them rose and swayed to the centre. They shed their cloaks to reveal young naked nymph–like girls, with gleaming, almost slug–like skins, swirling and entwining in an erotic dance ritual that intensified with the momentum of the chanting.

89

Not far away the maidens of the Rain Queen immersed
in their mesmerising snake dance. Clad only in loin
clothes and glistening with oil, forty–eight maidens, four
for every change of moon through the year, gathered in
a close line, each holding the elbows of the girl in front.
The gradual pumping action of their arms and legs
flowed across them in a wave. They hummed in a low
drone as the pulsating line moved around in a figure
eight. In the centre of each of the circles they travelled,
a staff projected from the ground snd had an apex
looped in the replication of coiled cobra.

The girls swayed their bodies and heads from side
to side and held their eyes closed in gathering
concentration. Each of them strained to find a sign that
could explain the plight of their kingdom. Many diviners
located themselves in private and solitary places in
rocky outcrops and thickets near the Royal Court to
search through their sacred tokens for the elusive clue.

Bakati, dejected, sought solace in consuming large
quantities of beer. He staggered aimlessly among the
performers muttering invectives at their efforts. Nobody
paid attention to him. He reached the Vatope site and
stood swaying, the erotic interplay of the naked dancers
entrancing him. Aroused, he stumbled away to find an
accommodating woman, only to collapse voiding in the
grass in an inebriated fugue.

As the night passed towards midnight the combined
efforts of the performers agitated the ancestral spirits into
action. One participant advantaged this situation like no
other; the mysterious and phantasmal Hosiyosiku. She
climbed to a high pinnacle of rock, where she lay on her
back and offered her majestic beauty for the indulgence
of the night spirits. It was to her, the Queen of the Night,
that they came to impart their transcendental exegesis.

Not long after dawn, the tired participants gathered
on the throne house terrace. Every inhabitant of the
settlement scrambled to witness the event. They climbed
trees, crammed on rooftops while some braved the
summits of the water tanks and crowded the approach
slope. The king had remained on his throne all night,
waiting. The councillors lay around. The attendants
brought food and drink.

Hosiyosiku threaded her way through the crowd. They
stood aside to let her pass. All had heard about the
legendary Queen of the Night, but few had ever seen
her. Even those who claimed they had, were never sure
whether it was merely an apparition or a figment of their
superstitious imaginations. But now she stood in reality
for all to behold – their apprehension at her presence
dismissed any doubt.

Posed prominently in front of the throne dais, she hailed
the king. A susurration of intrigue rippled

through the assembly. Some found it hard to reconcile that she actually existed, having always assumed her to be nothing more than a rumour. Whatever their opinions, it was impossible to ignore her beauty and majestic stature beneath the swirl of white plumes as a unique faint rustle of beads and rattle of gold bracelets wafted around her.

King Taba beckoned her to approach him on the throne dais. She mounted the terrace at the foot of the throne and looked steadily at King Taba – everyone tensed in silent anticipation.

She spoke in a clear husky voice. Taba leant forward and listened.

O, mighty king of the Sabiluto, I am the one called Hosiyosiku. I heed your call and feel your pain. To the Spirits of the Night, I have turned for guidance. They have responded with a message.

They have told me of an evil spirit–being who had been confined at the bottom of a mighty river where the First–of–All–Spirits, Mtombo, had banished him for his tyranny. But the river dried, allowing the evil–being to escape. He has subjugated many people since, but they have all perished under his authority. In the Sabiluto, because of their resilience to disease and their diverse abilities, he sees a new quarry.

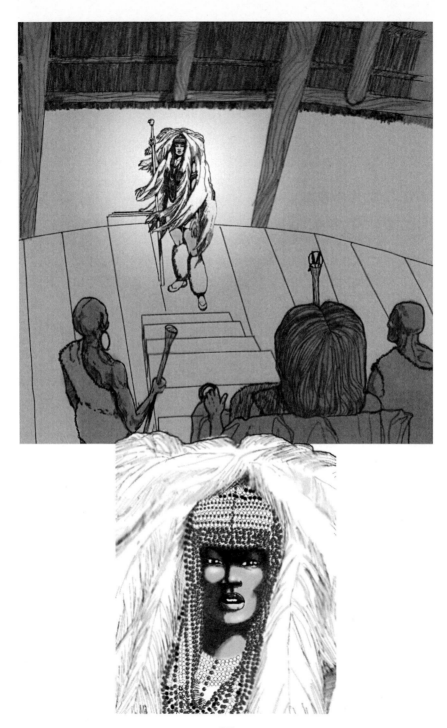

The Spirits of the Night say that if I call his
name, he will be forced to reveal himself and his
intentions.

I will only do this with your approval, my liege.
But I would be dishonest if I did not express my
apprehension at the outcome – I fear the truth will
be awesome.

The gathering murmured nervously at the prospect of
meeting such a force at close quarters.

The king raised his hand.
Hosiyosiku, if what you say is true, then it be better
to know what to expect, than to live with this
threatening cloud, not knowing what attrition will
be thrust upon us next. We must see this evil for
ourselves. I ask you, queen of the night, summon
this evil – call him now.

Hosiyosiku stepped towards the throne platform's edge
to face the vista of the plateau beyond the gathering
and raised her arms above her head, holding her
staff. Her cloak of long white feathers billowed with a
suspended sigh.

She launched into her invocation.
O, demon spirit, hear me – reveal yourself to me and
the Sabiluto, that we may see for ourselves what
manner of beast you are.

I call your name –

– VENGA

– VENGA

– VENGA

A breeze ruffled her feathers in a gentle
acknowledgment of her invective. Then, without
warning a roaring wind engulfed the hill – it came
from nowhere. Opaque gritty dust raced around them,
ripping off clothing, stinging and abrading skin, and
tossing lighter people around.

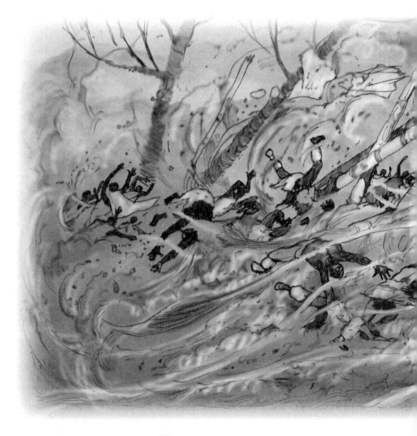

The diminutive Vatope swirled in the dust as if they were dry leaves.

The throne house structure groaned under the cyclonic rage as thatching and bearers flew away. The huge supporting poles buckled, snapped and crashed to the ground. Splinters and shards from their shattered breaks hurtled around like uncontrolled spears, mercilessly skewering and cutting through flesh.

It stopped.

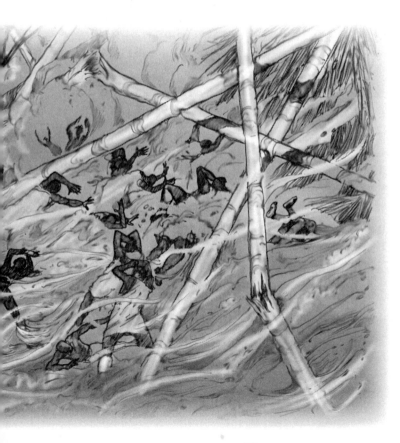

The sound of choking coughs and moans resonated through the opaqueness. As the dust settled a giant shimmering apparition of an enormous and powerful man with a black and white beard flowing from his face loomed above them. A black and white striped headdress hung low over his head and folded onto his shoulder, horns protruded above his forehead. His bright yellow eyes gleamed from an angry frown.

 The numinous phantom held its muscular arms out each side, they stretched the entire width of the assembly terrace. The startled people gazed up in frozen fear at the sight.

The eerie voice boomed through sharpened teeth,
It is me that you seek – I am the mighty spirit Venga.

Solitary, near naked and dust covered, Hosiyosiku rose from the entangled debris to confront the ominous spirit hovering above her. Her cloak of feathers, ripped from her body. Only a few dishevelled fragments of feathers remain fixed to her headdress and costume of beads.

Hosiyosiku demanded with a raised hand.
Reveal to me, great monster of destruction, your true intentions – tell us the truth of your presence.

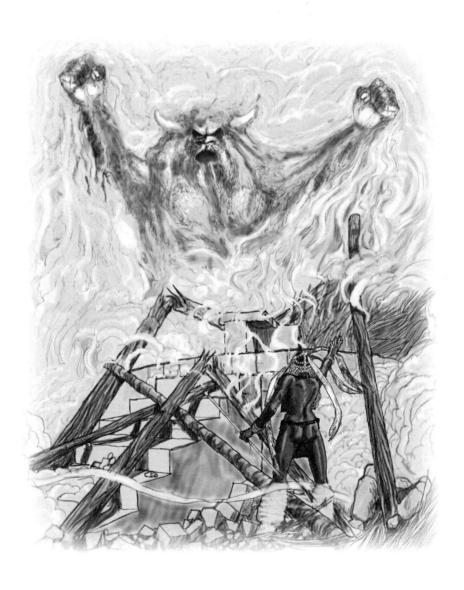

Droning words replied,

You feeble insignificant dogs, listen to your destiny. By the time the next rains have passed. I shall return as your god–king. You will worship no other spirit but Venga. Your pathetic idyllic ways are over. You have only one purpose in life; serving Venga.

Under my guards you will toil for me.

Your pathetic women will work – no longer wasting time with domesticity. They will labour in the fields, in the quarries and my buildings, and provide any pleasure I choose. Upon this very place, you will build for me a citadel of stone. Those who walk the parapets will be glorified; those who defy me will be cast into the hollows below to live in dark purgatory. And even after death their spirits will remain sealed in their cold stony tombs – forever.

Prepare yourselves. – prepare for my return, dogs of the Engelibizo. There is no escape or solution. You are mine. Prepare – prepare – prepare…

The malevolent spectre sucked away through the feculent ambience.

Potonoka and Otasa with guardsmen assisting rummaged among the thatching to find Taba.

Potonoka reached him first. He had been badly shaken but unharmed.

My king, are you hurt? Are you alright?

Taba muttered as he angrily disentangling himself from the thatching.

Umph! Yes, I am alright!. Find Hosiyosiku — bring her to me.

Hosiyosiku climbed up the platforms to him and knelt beside him, wiping the grime form her ebony face and upper arms.

Taba turned to her. Despair crimped his face. His voice quivered in anxiety.

He gripped her arm and blurted out.

Queen of the Night what can be done to protect us from this power. How can we save ourselves? Where can we go?

Hosiyosiku rubbed his hand reassuringly.

Venga has the power of the wind. He can frighten the animals to do his bidding. And, we have seen his wind storms and dust devils amusing themselves among the devastation, the dead and the dying — we have seen them crush the people to dust in their midst.

She pointed above her head, assertive.

But there remains the power of water and fire, neither of which is under Venga's power."

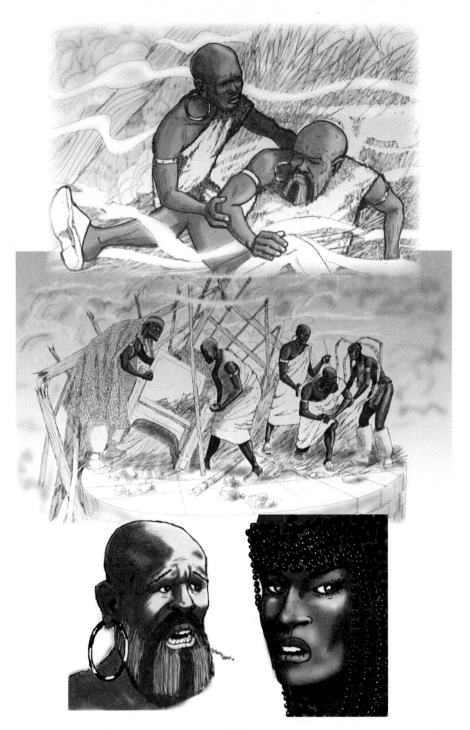

She managed a reassuring smile. "You have used the power of water with success already against the dust devils, and the terrified animals.

She paused. Many bedraggled Sabiluto had gathered around to hear her revelation.

As fire and water served to drive the elephant attack from the Royal Court, then it is to these powers we must turn.

Taba looked at her helplessly.

How do we do this, Hosiyosiku? We are mere mortals.

Hosiyosiku stood erect and defiant.

The First of All Spirits, Mtombo, controls everything, spiritual and mortal. But we are unable to reach him directly; we must seek out his agents, my King.

Taba shook his head as he asked,

Who are these agents? I have no knowledge of such people.

Hosiyosiku raised her chin.

That is only because you have never had need of them. Now you do. One such agent is Nyamanzi, Queen of the Engelibizo waterways. She is a servant of the Great Water Spirit, Vuro. But her arrogance presents a problem – perhaps not the best approach to start with.

I would have to make some token gesture to attract her attention.

Then there is Chetemoto, the Fire Goddess or Commander of Fire. Now she has the direct ear of Mtombo and in turn his control over fire and the rain. She would be able to guide the way. Nyamanzi would probably follow her lead but never admit it, though.

Taba shook his head with a degree of doubt.
Where is Chetemoto — where can we find her?

Hosiyosiku turned her face to the sky and again pointed upwards.
She lives in the supernatural space above the Tabezulu, so far away from here, I fear the Sabiluto have never ventured there.

The Spirits of the Night told me that there are those who know the way. We should go to them without delay.

Journey to the Sky

When the dust eventually cleared from the air, the black cloud on the horizon transformed into a Goliath image of Venga, hovering in intense vigilance, and visible from every part of the plateau. At night its eyes glowed. Only low swooping rain clouds brought respite from the awesome surveillance but on their departure it resumed.

Once the council chamber had been cleared of debris and builders initiated reconstruction of the roof, the activity in the councillors below continued. Several days later they again sat on their benches.

Hosiyosiku, scantily clad in her beads, bracelets and remaining plumage, stood at the entrance to the chamber to address the council.

My King and Councillors, it is best that I lead the search for Chetemoto. I"m familiar with the swamps and the Vatope people, some of whom are here among us, and willing to assist in our venture through the swamps. They have already sent messengers back to prepare their people for our arrival. We"ll have to cross the swamps to reach the Tabezulu.

Without the Vatope, there will be little chance of success. The beasts, leaches, snakes and multitude of other predators, seldom seen by

the Sabiluto, would consume the searchers before
they could reach halfway across.

Her attire hissed its curious rustle.
Venga will be upon this place soon after the rains
have passed and there's nothing you can do to
prevent it. Submission to his influence will be your
only course then, to wait for whatever Chetemoto
has to predict.

How long this will take, I can not say.

She turned her elegant face sagaciously to the roof.
For me, it would be wiser to leave before Venga
arrives. He will not treat my fearless confrontation
of him with favour. I can do more in the hidden
spaces of the wetlands.

Venga's magic has no power there. Only his men
could enter, but they, like any mortal, would be
subject to the vagaries of the swamps.

With Hosiyosiku and the remaining Vatope directing
the way, Councillors and brothers Potonoka and
Otasa set out with a company of Royal Guards, porters
and attendants, totalling one hundred, towards the
Tabezulu, until then, a distant blue smudge on the
horizon to even the most widely travelled Sabiluto.

With no home or family left, Hunter Tela and his young brother Gono joined the searchers. Tela's reputation as a skilled hunter and scout made him a popular participant in the venture.

Intermittent diurnal showers kept the plains moist, bringing partial relief to devastation through which they passed. En route, they encountered many villagers busy reconstructing their damaged settlements. Calls of encouragement and support greeted them and food and clothing were brought to them – far more than they could transport. All but the protecting Royal Guard on the flanks carried two packs suspended from the shoulders while those who had joined the party specifically as porters carried additional chest and backpacks

Tela and Gono displayed alert caution towards every wild animal they encountered, which could present a danger with their own recent experiences still dominated their minds.

Hosiyosiku ascertained that Venga's dust devils were inoperable in wet conditions as they relied on the dry earth and grass for their sustenance and growth. With temporary confidence installed, she led the Sabiluto searchers behind the green trail of diminutive Vatope to the fluvian expanses of the swamplands.

It took a month before they reached the brink of the escarpment that descended to the swamps. Standing on the edge of the depression, she viewed the feature that stretched across the horizon. Patches of water reflected through the endless carpet of dense verdant foliation.

With a graceful arm extended and ringed in tinkling gold bracelets, she pointed to the swamplands.
There, only there, in the wetlands is it safe from the power of Venga. There, I"ll remain until it is time — I have no choice. Were Venga to find me and subjugate me, I fear the path that I have opened to establish a retaliation through Chetemoto would be destroyed.

The next morning, still following their Vatope guides, they snaked their descent to the swamp through thickening undergrowth that exuded wafts of humus–laden redolence as each step compressed the damp surface.

Avifauna and insects proliferated around them with incrementing resonance. At the edge of the water, a group of the strange taciturn Vatope, hovering magically on the surface, were there to meet them and their returning brethren.
Hosiyosiku descended alone to greet them and receive her instructions.

She clambered back up to the searchers.
The Vatope beckon us to follow. We must obey their directions without question if we're to traverse the swamps successfully.

As the Sabiluto eased their way down the bank to the swamp water, the Vatope dispersed themselves through the string of Sabiluto travellers to prevent anyone straying in the arduous conditions.

A labyrinth of humid marshes confronted them, often fog bound. Reeds and tenebrous waterways flooded beneath dark undergrowth to provide sanctuary for the voracious beasts that lived there: constrictor ophidians as thick as a man's leg, irascible hippo, crocodile and fish, the size of a man, with panther–like teeth – all participants on

the continuing cycle of violence. The mantra of "kill or be killed" dominated the swamplands.

They struggled through the muddy water, unyielding and cutting reeds, under the constantly monitoring of hungry crocodiles and inimical hippopotami. Then leaches attached themselves to every bit of flesh – thousands of them squirming towards this new offering of sustenance.

The Vatope knew how to dislodge them with sprinklings of a white powder – only a sparse application proved enough to detach the blood–suckers, and a salve rubbed over the broken skin prevented infection in the dank noisome environment. The Vatope and Hosiyosiku displayed immunity to the hostilities of the swamps. Predators froze with consternation at their presence and the leaches left them alone.

The Vatope appeared to glide across the terrain as if supported on cushions of air, hardly ruffling the surface of the water or foliage. Hosiyosiku skimmed along in effortless strides. The Sabiluto, despite their greater stature, struggled with the pace.

Although the Sabiluto were familiar with the Vatope, they nevertheless remained an enigma, maintaining there distance in the inhospitable swamps. It was speculated that they had descended from a people, the Sandmen, who once inhabited the central deserts of the old Africa, but no one knew for sure; not even the Vatope

The Vatope.

The Vatope were best known as the suppliers of the Royal Guard's cloaks. The small Vatope hunted the ferocious giant swamp dragon with a vengeance, determined to return it to the extinction from which it miraculously appeared one hundred fifty years before. As in all previous dragons, it had huge lungs and as it breathed and roared in the dank wetland air it emitted clouds of condensation, adding to its spectacle.

The Vatope cloaks were also of the swamp dragon skin, which, when after special curing only known to the Vatope, resisted cutting from blades and penetration from arrows, and when wrinkled, rustled with a distinct susurrus. The cloak, although warm, breathed in the heat to provide a most amazing garment and a privilege to own.

Each year, those Royal Guard graduates who were not in line to receive a cloak from a retiring Guard, travelled to a place at the edge of the Engelibizo Plateau were the Vatope displayed the latest cloaks they had made, hanging them on frames. They disappeared before the graduates arrived – and always supplied the exact number required. This goodwill gesture had been enacted for as long as the swamp dragon had emerged, and, despite killing everyone they came across, the reptiles never seemed to abate.

Killing the swamp dragon had developed into a definitive accomplishment. On discovering the beast, the Vatope would entice it into a chase, directed towards an established location of quicksand. The Vatope could glide across the surface, but the dragon became bogged. A swift manoeuvre secured its tale to a rope noose.

The Vatope waited as the lumbering animal struggled in the grasping quicksand until it sank, exhausted. Using a gantry and counterweights contained in a sack, they would drag the dragon onto solid ground, usually near a precipice. The gantry was erected against a precipice high enough to to pull the dragon to its a full length and suspend it above a spike, which was positioned below its open mouth.

With a command the hoist rope would be disengaged from the counter weight, dropping the beast onto spike where it would be impaled and bleed to death. The Vatope could find no reason to be merciful. Over the years the swamp dragons had killed and maimed too many of their number for any consciousness to have relevance.

Once deceased, they would skin and dissect it and as its flesh was palatable it was quickly consumed with any excess cured into a tasty jerky – and, of course, they cured the coveted skin.

The searchers emerged from the swamps worse for wear and were happy to take a deserved rest near a river. Their Vatope guides left them after indicating the direction to the foothills of the mighty Tabezulu.

They gathered their camp under the immense spreading branches of an enormous ficus tree at the edge of clear stream. Beyond the stream, not far from the bank, a wall of foliage announced the beginning of the forest region that spread to the foothills of the Tabezulu Mountains that reached beyond the clouds in mystical ascendancy.

Hosiyosiku addressed the Sabiluto before she left.
Once you have located Chetemoton, she will deliver her edict and prepare you for future events. I have no knowledge of what this might be or how long it will take, but I am sure that it will involve me and other agents of the spirit world.

She paused and dropped her eyes,
Also, I must warn you that the road to liberty for the Sabiluto will be treacherous and at times seemingly pointless, but the result will fortify your nation as never before.

Go well, brave men of the Sabiluto, and be worthy of your name – fear nothing.

She stood for a moment, looking at the searchers with solemnity, before her image faded and vanished – the Sabiluto were alone.

After a few days rest, the search party ventured forward, passing through spaces overgrown with giant plants and ferns – places an species none of them had ever seen before. Ahead in the distance above a forest of tall trees the vast mountains ascended into the clouds in a cerulean stain across the horizon. They gathered on a rise that broke above the undergrowth to examine the enormous feature.

Potonoka sighed, unable to disguise his despair at the enormity of the task confronting them. His eyes fixed on the mountains.

He sighed.
    Ah! The Mountains of the Sky – somewhere up there we have to try and find Chetemoto.

The others shared his pessimism but Otasa took his brother's elbow, drew him from his despondency.

He walked him forward with accentuated and comical goose steps.
    Come my brother, with each step the goal draws closer.

Looking at the vertical obstacle confronting them.

He added.
    The mountains cannot be like this for their entire length – we will find a way.

129

Otasa's antics forced a sliver of a smile from Potonoka as he paced next to brother down the slope towards their objective.

A week later they reached the forest of tall trees. Aghast, their gaze roamed the spectacle. No imagination could have prepared them for the enormity of the trees. Their trunks, so thick that the spans of eight men could not reach around the base of the smallest and they climbed out of sight, beyond the mantle of rustling leaves.

Dwarfed, the Sabiluto advanced into the dismal interior. Strings of sun rays pierced through to light the undergrowth in shimmering pools, but away from their vicinity, visibility dimmed dramatically. The pungent smell of dank humus filled their nostrils. Most ferns grew above shoulder height forcing the men to close their ranks until they progressed in two shoulder-to-shoulder columns.

Orders were given not to leave stragglers and to halt the column should anyone fall behind. Unfamiliar rustling in the bushes around them indicated the presence of wildlife. They could not see them and, presuming them to be large snakes or lizards, their tension soared.

As they advanced, the ground climbed, announcing
the advent of the foothills, which inclined and levelled
in a series of terraces with deer and wild pig plentiful.

Otasa commented casually on seeing an abundance
of wild pigs two–hundred paces away,
We haven't had fresh meat for sometime.

Tela, standing close by, heard his comment.

Otasa turned to engage Tela..
Do you think...

But in an instant, Tela had fired an arrow, striking a
grazing pig in the side of the head. It slumped dead on
its stomach without a sound, as a second arrow dropped
another pig.

Everyone who witnessed the performance gasped as
few had seen a display of marksmanship to equal it.

All the way, Tela instructed Gono in toxophily with the
large powerful bow, although Gono's arms were not
long enough or strong enough to fully draw back an
arrow.

While choosing targets at random for Gono to fire at,
usually a tree, he repeated directives to his young
brother.
**Bring the arrow into the aim as you pull it back – in
one movement. Practise this before accuracy.**

With each shot, Gono's skill accrued.

Days passed until the end of the cascading plateaus
heralded excited calls from the front; they had
encountered a wall of rock. From it the mountains
disappeared vertically passed the trees into the clouds.
There appeared no possibly way up the feature.

Otasa suggested.
I think we should rest here and make some plans.

Potonoka agreed and the men rapidly prepared a
clearing.

By mid–afternoon the Sabiluto had settled into a camp
routine. Wood had been gathered and three fires with
rudimentary spits were organized as others hoisted
the pigs up by their hind quarters and began skinning
them, taking care not to waste a single morsel of the
precious meat. The prospect of a hot meal of fresh pork,
the first in weeks, lifted their spirits.

The men gathered in files under the supervision of
the Sabiluto guards as flashing sound of knives being
sharpened heralded the meal. The men had gathered
leaves as makeshift plates upon which slivers of
the grilled pork were laid with reverence. Laughter
and banter drifted through the forest along with the
appetising aroma of the cooking meat.

Like a wafting harbinger it reached the senses of the forest dwellers.

The Mathiops

Mathiop" was a portmanteau word of Homo aethiops, resulting from a bizarre biological experiment several centuries before to determine the origins of the human race. The Technos destined the Mathiops for extermination when the results of the DNA recombinant experiments were deemed to have failed, without reaching a defining answer.

Although barely waist-high to the average adult human, the Mathiops displayed an exceptional intellect which they used to plea-bargained for their survival. They opted to be abandoned in the most inaccessible and inhospitable place their creators could locate.

VTOL transporters dropped fifty of them at the edge of the forest of gigantic tress in the vast wilderness of Nova Afrika. Other mutants that had survived abandoned cloning experiments accompanied the deportation.

The forests had a reputation for harbouring the most viscous primates and carnivores to have emerged from the Green Evolution. The Technos considered the Mathiops chance of survival improbable.

137

The Mathiops concealed from the Technos, their
possession of an innate memory bank covering
millennia. Their exceptional knowledge base, combined
with remarkable agility, helped them survive and
propagate to a secure number and they rapidly
mastered the forest domain, having destroyed or driven
out most of the hostile predators.

As an entity they were mostly congenial in their
behaviour, barring their hatred for Technos, and spoke
in a refined Uneng accent, in a complete discord to their
animalistic appearance. They rejected all technology
except for the most rudimentary that was considered
necessary for survival.

They dressed in the cured skins of the primates they
hunted as adversaries to their domain. and wore briefs
cured from the hide of the snow panther with the
tail attached,. Their genetic coding had inexplicably
dropped off their tails, so they reckoned the snow
panther's tail would be a cute accessory. Their diet
also included birds, snakes, deer and a variety of fruit
and nuts.

The bow and arrow emerged as their favourite weapon.
The bow, with large curls at each end, assisted them
to swing between branches of the high canopy, where
they spent most of their time. With the hoops of the bows
linked together they could form long chains long chains,
which allowed them to forest floor. Walking upright

scurry back and forth from the was not a comfortable experience due to their prehensile feet, which limited them to a loping sprint over short distances.

Net weaving developed into another prominent skill. They used nets prolifically in hunting and as safety measures beneath their communes, especially where infants existed. Individuals were often seen snaring birds with their nets as the birds flew between trees high in the canopy.

They were industrious builders and created large comfortable timber platforms around the sturdy trunks of the massive trees above the mid-level of the forest foliation. Deep pitched roofs of split bamboo covered the living areas protecting them from the daily dousing of rain that occurred in the afternoons. Sturdy ropes linked the platforms to provide a convenient articulated network and many of the dwellings had nets below and between them.

A century earlier some Mathiops developed a method of hang gliding and decided to leave the forest to search for a life style high in the mountains where their skill would dominate. These people became known as the Khuda mountain people. The two groups only met on rare occasions.

The Technos also left a rather morose collection of mutant cannibals to a quick fate in the forest, the

Taals, who resembled Neanderthal, but they too managed to survive beyond expectations. Many Mathiops fell victim to them over time. And, although the Taals had dwindled to a point of extinction, the isolated remnant communities still posed a threat to the unwary.

Then there was the Mathiops coming–of–age ritual.

A young Mathiop male scurried on all fours through the undergrowth, playing a dangerous game. He had reached adulthood and opted to earn his pants, made from the rear–quarter hide of the snow panther, with the tail attached.

Although they shot and trapped the snow panther regularly, the pants chase had been a long –standing tradition for young adult males to prove their mettle on reaching puberty – and it was from a snow panther that this young Mathiop now ran.

The snow panther, a medium–size cat but much larger than a Mathiop, had a thick off–white coat with subtle blotch markings. It had an accentuated aggression, inimitable speed and agility, and a preference for Mathiops as a dietary delicacy.

In turn, the Mathiops considered the snow panther a culinary delight, and coveted its pelt, not only as a symbol of male bravado but also as a betrothal

140

gift by males to their intended partners. Fortunately for the snow panther, it proved difficult to hunt, capture or kill and as a prolific breeder it maintained its numbers.

The snow leopard had mastered hunting in the forest as well as on the steep mountain slopes and often ventured high into the snow–covered peaks and the sanctuary of the mountain goat.

The young Mathiop could sense the snow panther gaining on him. Its closing presence formulated his plan: he purposely presented himself as a quarry for the cat, enticing it into a chase. Normally the panther's cunning prevented it falling for simple tricks so the alternative strategy involved a ruse that appeared to offer an easy kill for the leopard.

But the timing had to be perfect with only thirty yards of sprinting in the whole process and no margin for error. Initiating the enactment required the Mathiop to drop from a low branch, attached to a rope, about twenty paces in front of the panther then feign a fall, roll around and clutch a leg, yelping.

Realising the advantage of an injured Mathiop on the ground a short distance away the snow panther, more often than not, would be unable to resist an attack. In an instant, the Mathiop dashed for a predetermined point of the trap with the speeding animal in pursuit.

The rope that tied to the fleeing Mathiop linked to a log weight that other Mathiops slipped off two parallel branches high in the canopy at the start of the chase, tensing the rope and pulling the young Mathiop along as he sprinted.

With the panther less than ten paces behind and preparing to leap forward the rope reached the end of its play and yanked the Mathiop aloft. The young males practised this manoeuvre to perfection. The momentum swept him up as the panther jumped as extended claws whizzed passed his feet – he jerked his knees up just in time. The panther landed in the centre of a net.

Mathiops dropped from the canopy each gripping the end of a rope looped around branches and attached to the net. As they descended the ropes yanked the net upward, engulfing the panther. The panther's berserk response soon entangled it in the mesh until it hung twisted up, snarling and caterwauling.

More Mathiops attached to ropes, plunged form the foliation to surround the scene. A large male slipped down the rope a bow with a quiver of arrows and handed them to the young participant. He carefully selected and arrow and raised it into the aim before pulling back the bow string and shooting an arrow into the snow panther's brain.

A resounding cheer of, "Pants, pants, pants," resonated through the forest but the young Mathiop sensed remorse at seeing the magnificent feline slumped in its entangled demise – he doubted that he would ever excel as a hunter.

But their celebration was halted as a shrill, eerie, almost indiscernible whistle emanated form within the forest's extensive compages – a signal for immediate and present danger.

As swiftly as they had descended, the Mathiops hauled themselves and the panther into the mantle to squester themselves in silence. Only a trickle of blood droplets fell onto a fern below, flicking the fronds in a subdued encore to the earlier action. Above, round attentive eyes snatched around the forest to establish the nature of the threat.

A hiss from a Mathiop turned attention in one direction. From the gloom, they saw two large figures wading through the undergrowth – humans, large humans, wearing green capes that whispered as they moved.

They had dark complexions and bald heads contained in red headbands. They parted and cut back the foliage with stout spears as the progressed to allow others to followed several paces behind them. The Mathiops slipped away to confer.

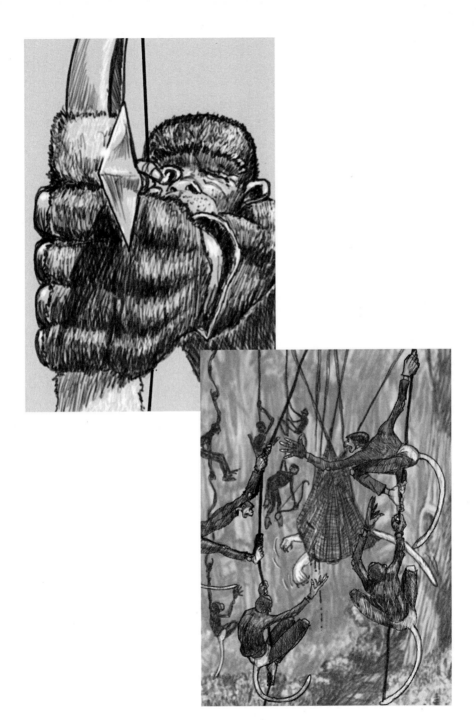

In the morning Potonoka and Otasa prepare a plan and explained their decision to the men. Seated on stools in in their makeshift headquarters with Tela and Gono seated cross legged before him,

Pontonopka delivered his plan.

Tela, I want you to establish a temporary camp here. See what fresh food, you and Gono can find and bring it to the camp.

Being familiar with Tela's skill, whose outstanding accuracy had already brought down several more wild bore and deer to refresh their supplies, he had little doubt that fresh meat supplies would be adequate.

I will leave twenty men here, including five guardsmen.

Otasa and I will divide the rest of the group into two groups of forty and go in opposite directions along the cliff face to find a way up. We will travel for five days, then return to this point, unless something transpires. If that should happen we will send runners to find the other group and bring them back to this point.

He rubbed his chin between his thumb and forefinger as he considered his next instruction.

I think we should start his exercise without delay.

149

Two days out, the lead scouts of Otasa's group raised their hands to halt them. The other guards automatically took up their defensive positions along the flanks. A scout beckoned Otasa forward.

Two strange and diminutive figures stood before them. Barely waist–high to the Guardsmen, they looked like monkeys, yet their faces and posture possessed impish human characteristics.

 They were a male and a female and each carried a bow with accentuated curled ends. Otasa could not discern whether they wore animal pelts or they had hirsute hides.

The male smiled at the Sabiluto, unafraid, indicating a desire to make contact, while his partner stood peering around him with less bravado and big anxious eyes. Their feet were large and prehensile.

Otasa stepped closer and raised his open right hand in greeting. The monkey–man copied his gesture, showing a hand with long fingers and an opposing thumb, unlike most other primates.

The creature spoke first in pellucid and accented Uneng.
Greetings my good man. Welcome to our forest.

The clarity of the monkey–man's diction amazed Otasa. He could only stammer a reply.
Thank you, and, and greetings to you. We come in peace. We offer no harm. We merely seek an oracle...

The small creature replied.
No need to explain, we have been monitoring your progress for sometime and have overheard much of your conversations.

You are Councillor Otasa of the Sabiluto, is that not so?

Otasa muttered a response.
I am – you surprise me.

The monkey–man pulled the female from behind and stood her beside him.
Well, I am Principal Don of the Mathiops, and this is my lady, Edna.

I am the elected leader of the Mathiops and offer any assistance we can in your quest. We waited until you had split up into smaller groups, just in case you reacted aggressively to our approach, and you did not have that wretched archer with you – the one you call Tela. He would have surely dropped us before we could make contact. His skill is so remarkable and so powerful it makes our tiny bows seem feckless.

From your discourse, we have also established you to be an honourable race – from the plains, I presume.

Otasa could not suppress a smile at the extraordinary exchange.

Yes we are from the Engelibizo Plateau and we seek the council of an oracle named Chetemoto.

Principal Don murmured.

Chetemoto, you say. Yes, we have heard of such a witch from our cousins, the Khuda. They live high up in mountains but drop in from time to time.

He chuckled at his humour.

They can fly, you see.

Otasa, did not fully grasp the issue, but chuckled anyway.

Oh yes, I see.

During their discussion, the rest of the Sabiluto had gathered around, towering above the Mathiop couple, absorbed in intrigue.

Principal Don explained.

You are the first humans that we have encountered, since the Technos abandoned us in this forest – um, let me see....

He rubbed his chin in thought.

Edna blurted out.

It's been two hundred and fourteen years. Six months and twenty–one days.

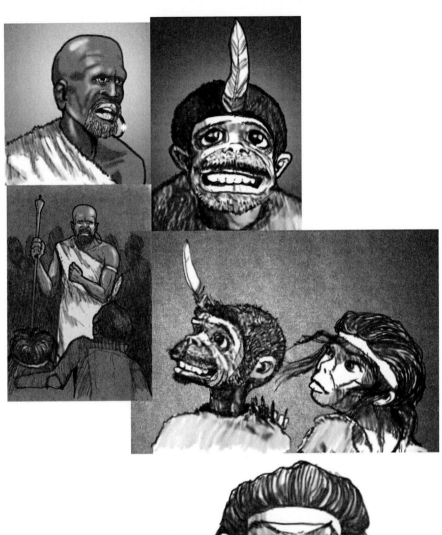

She braced herself with a satisfied grin.

Don laughed at her calculation.
And don't doubt her she's never wrong.

Otasa had no response. His cerebral adjudication of the peculiar creatures had jumped into advanced mode, but no conclusion was forthcoming.

Principal Don must have sensed his bemusement.
Perhaps you should meet some of our people.

He waived his arm around the scene,
To reassure you that this truly is our forest and that we are as friendly as you yourselves claim to be.

Don turned his face up to the forest mantle, spread his arm high and called out.
Greet our friends from the plains, Mathiops – greet the Sabiluto.

In a spontaneous burst the entire surroundings erupted in a chorus of,
Sabiluto, Sabiluto.

The foliage shook in every direction and figures leaped between branches. Loose leaves fluttered down in a sparkling shower. A deluge of Mathiops slid down the massive tree trunks while others lowered themselves down in catenated strings, using their bows as links while others dropped ropes and scrambled down.

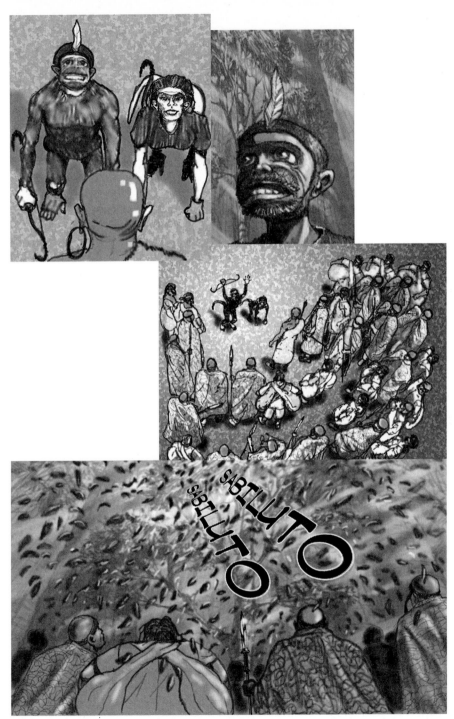

157

They swarmed around the searchers and continued chanting in loud unison.

Sabiluto, Sabiluto, Sabiluto.

Soon the cascading glittering green leaves covered them as the forest people swirled between the Sabiluto, touching their clothes and hands as they passed and gelled them in a waist–high pool of gaiety.

The next day Principal Don led Otasa to a fissure about three–feet wide in the cliff face. It split the entire height of the vertical rock.

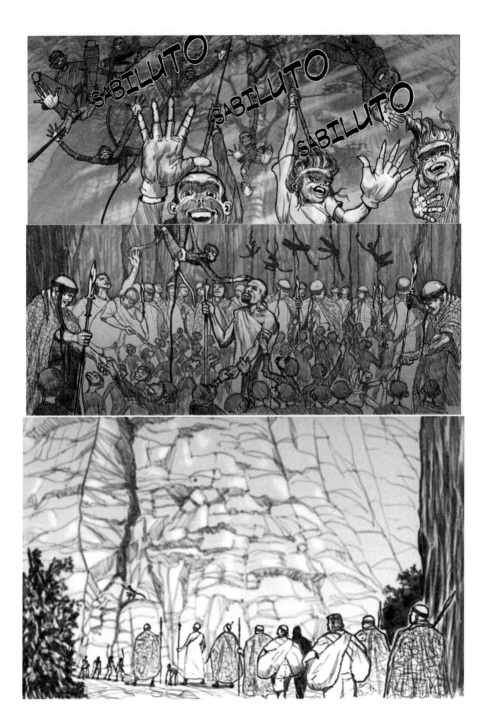

159

After examining the fissure, Otasa gave instructions to
a runner who had accompanied them.

Get Tela to relocate the camp at this place in front
of the fissure then find Potonoka and tell him to return to this place immediately and await our return.

He pointed into the fissure,

I will take twenty men and climb to meet the Khuda
mountain people.

The runner darted away. Some Mathiops tried keeping
up with his progress his through the mantle but he soon
out distanced them.

While they waited for Tela, Otasa selected a pool of
sunlight where a large tree trunk had fallen. He stood
authoritatively and statuesque next to the trunk holding
his staff, and looked around the area of massive trees
and undergrowth.

He knew that the Mathiops were looking at him.
His white robe gleamed in contrast to his ebony
complexion. Each time he moved his head a glitter of
light sparked from his earring.

The pale palm and white nails of his fingers were like
a mesmerising beacon as he waved the Mathiops to
close around him.

Mathiops, I need to explain our presence here.
Please gather around. I want to tell you this first
hand to avoid any misunderstandings and gossip.
We must be united — please gather around.

Otasa sat on the trunk to wait. Some Mathiops perched on the trunk beside him as other sat around at a respectful distance in silent expectancy, almost reverent of the stranger who exuded such authority and wisdom. Principal Don and Edna weaved through the gathering to sit together in front of him.

Otasa began his discourse.

Dear friends of this most magnificent forest, we of the plains are not here by choice sadly but through a catastrophe that has ravanged the plains beyond recognition. We are indeed lucky survivors.

Our land has been subjugated by an evil behemoth. This monster is called Venga and he is a spirit being that has escaped incarceration imposed by our Lord Mtombo. Venga has the command over the wind, which he uses to terrify and control wild animals into committing uncharacteristic attacks against humans. He also creates dust devils that chase and pulverize our people and anything else in their path.

He paused to let the significance of his introduction filter into the cognition of his audience. All eyes focused upon him.

Through the amazing gifts of our diviners and the wonderful and magnificent Hosiyosiku, Queen of the Night, we were able to evoke Venga to deliver his intentions and they were dire.

162

Total subjugation was the only criteria.

But from this Hosiyosiku evolved a plan. She realized that although Venga's power was immense, it was yet limited as he had no command over fire or water and we had proved their significance while confronting his onslaught.

Acting on Hosiyosuku's advice, she suggested we consult with an oracle called Chetemoto who has the command over fire and is in the confidence of the Lord Mtombo.

Excatly what it is she can do for us is not known at this stage, but we need any help we can get to combat this massive degradation of our dignity.

Principal Don placed his hand to mouth in a gesture of concern.
But Coiuncillor Otasa what is to prevent this Venga from reaching us here in the forest? What can we do?

Otasa flashed an assuaging palm.
The swamps – Venga cannot reach you over the swamps. He can send human minions such as an army, but he cannot reach you himself. Where there is water aplenty his power is quelled or so the diviners tell us.

Principal Don stood; Edna rose beside him.
Then we must play our part. It appears to me
that this threat is as much against us as it is to
anyone alive in this whole place.

He raised his hand in a salutation.
Councillor Otasa, we pledge our absolute support.
As diminutive as we are, you will soon learn that
our perspicacity is not something with which to be
trifled.

The gathering of Mathiops stood up in unified support
of Don's proclamation. They all realised that the threat
Otasa revealed could reach far beyond the plains.

Tela's group arrived, contained in a garrulous pool of
Mathiops and set about establishing a camp, with ample
assistance from the industrious little forest dwellers.

Their expertise in construction, using forest materials
soon became evident. As soon as convenient, Otasa
gathered his team, equipping them with as much
supplies as he thought necessary to negotiate the
difficult terrain ahead.

In a single file he led the column into the darkness of
the crevice. After a short distance, broken rubble and
boulders filled the spaces forcing them to use all fours
as they began their ascent. Hands, knees and elbows
rapidly lacerated on the sharp fractured surfaces. The
climbers utilized any

available piece of clothing they could avail as protection. The cleavage narrowed, only allowing enough space for a single man to negotiate the tenebrous and claustraphopic ascent.

Some of the larger guardsmen found the space arduous, almost trapping them as they attempted to squeeze through. A few had to climb higher to find the space to slither through. It gave Otasa the notion to reconsider the selection of his team. He returned the bigger men back to Tela's camp to be replaced with more wiry porters.

Several Mathiops, under the leadership of one called Lod, had joined Otasa and scampered ahead to indicate the most accessible route. On passing Otasa, Lod told him that a small plateau occupied the top of the cliff, before the mountains sloped upwards into the clouds. The Sabiluto erected a temporary camp there.

Otasa sent a message down to Tela, telling him to make a more substantial camp on the small plateau once he had completed the main one on the forest floor. Otasa called the higher camp, Ingalane, after the Baqala name for a food storage hut built on poles to keep it clear of animals – except monkeys, of course. The Mathiops enjoyed the wit.

The Mathiops supervised the making of climbing ropes with shoulder loops every ten feet. The remaining guardsmen removed their swords from

167

their staffs and sheathed them, as they would need both hands for climbing.

The forest dwellers held little doubt that whatever climbing equipment and preparation the Sabiluto made it would not be enough. The daunting climb to seek Chetemoto commenced as soon as they felt ready.

Before the first day ended the temperature plummeted, augmenting the challenge of their mission. The Mathiops guides carefully selected the most accommodating route for the heftier warriors and laden porters, but even they could not prevent two men, one a porter and the other a guard, from slipping on the damp surface and falling over the edge of a narrow ledge in a wail of anguish.

Others gripped the rope and dropped to their haunches for more traction as it slithered over the edge quivered into tautness. They tried to to pull the rope back pushing their feet as they slowly slipped to the brink. Just in time, one man looped the rope around a rock to hold it firm. The fallen men dangled from their loops out of sight in the mist.

All attempts to reel in the rope failed. Further down it had wedged between two rocks and jammed. Lod and and some Mathiops clambered down as far as they could to help, but the mist blanketed visibility. The porter hung at the bottom, his heavy

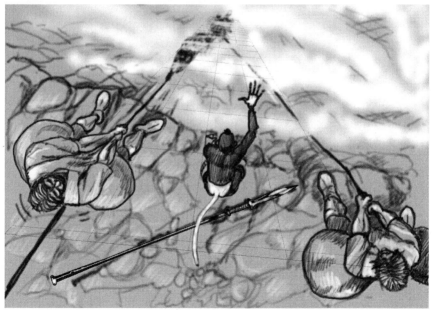

packs prevented him from making any attempt to climb up the rope.

The suspended guard called to him and reached into the opaqueness of the ten feet that separated them.

He urged.
Drop the packs – try and reach for me.

There was no response, only a gurgling sound.

A Mathiop's voice resonated through the fog.
I think the packs are strangling him,.

The Mathiop called down.
Hold on – I'm coming down.

The guard called back.
No – stay where you are – I'll go down to him.

The guard wriggled free of the loop and swung down the rope.

Lod reached the point where the rope had wedged in the rocks, but he could not pull it free. The weight of the two men and packs held it firm.

Lod announced into the mist to whoever was listening.
The rope is wedged between two rocks – it's too heavy to move.

The guard reached the porter. He wrapped his legs
around the rope and pushed against the rock face,
reached down and pulled the heavy packs over
the man's head – they fell into the opaque mist. The
guard maneuvred himself next to the porter and held
him tightly.

He called back to Lod.
The packs are free.

With his feet planted each side of the rope Lod griped
it and gave a mighty heave. It slipped free almost
flinging Lod away but he held on to shout.
It's free.

On the path above the rope slackened sending the men
who grasped it sprawling back, but they held their grip.

Otasa took charge and stood aside the men.

He yelled his command while peering over the edge.
Pull, pull – pull with all your might.

Under the constant encouragement of the Mathiops the
two men slowly emerged from the mist and toppled
over the edge of the cliff on to the path. The porter
needed attention, his breathing was rasping.

Lod looked up at Otatsa,
I think his ribs are broken.

Lod turned his attention to the gaurdsman slumped beneath his green cloak and examined his hands. They were bleeding and in places cut to the bone. Otasa realized their contribution was over.

He addressed the guard.
As carefully as you can manage, guard, take the porter back to Engalane. The rest of us will continue – with much added caution, I might add.

Lod rummaged in one of the bags to extract some ointment and linen bandages which he applied the ointment to the guard's injured hands.

Melancholy closed in with the mist. The experience of their first casualty manifested the concern as to how many more might they experience in their quest to reach Chetemoto.

Now clad in extra furs, they took every step forward with this added precaution. careful and unanimous cooperation became the mantra of their progress as they groped through the thickening white gloom for four days and nights, at times crawling further cutting and blistering already bleeding hands, feet and knees.

The vigilant Mathiops brushed back and forth their line in an encouraging caress, offering assurance and assistance wherever they could. In an untiring effort, they dispensed food, water and

medication from the porters' packs. Without them the Sabiluto might well have abandoned their mission at that early stage.

The Sabiluto staggered into a pool of daylight, where green fresh grass covered a gradually sloping area. Each man fell in grateful exhaustion onto the turf where they lay coughing and spluttering in the rarified air.

The Mathiops scurried around, chirping optimism. When the searchers eventually regained their composure the vista of endless mountain peaks projected through the clouds and spread into the sparkling distance.

Otatsa sat, slumped back on his arms. Lod knelt next to him and offered him some water from a hide bladder. He drank.

Lod pointed to a ridge arching above them.
Up there – by tomorrow evening – we will be in reach of the Khuda.

Otasa asked with a splutter.
Breathing – will it worsen as we climb?

Lod smiled.
The air will get worse, yes, but in a few days you will acclimatize. One morning you will awaken and wonder what all the fuss was about.

Otasa chortled at the jibe.

The next evening as they walked with leaden steps along a narrow ridge from nowhere, a large bird swooped over them. Startled, the guards flung off their rope loops and snatched at their swords.

'The Mathiops shouted and jumped up and down and waved their arms excitedly.

Stop, stop – don't be afraid – it's the Khuda.

They saw the bird loop back in the distance and glide towards them. As it approached they could discern that a small figure that hung below a large wing.

It circled and landed ahead of them. The wing folded around him in a cape as the Mathiops ran towards him, gesticulating and yelling happily. He detached the staffs from the wings, pulled them apart and held them together.

Lod informed Otasa that the Khuda flyer was called Teno. He was slightly smaller than his cousins the Mathiops, with smooth blue–black hue to his skin, and his features were more human than the Mathiops and, like his cousins, he spoke in lucid Uneng.

Lod and Otasa scrambled to explain the purpose of the unusual visit that the Sabiluto have made to their lofty kingdom.

178

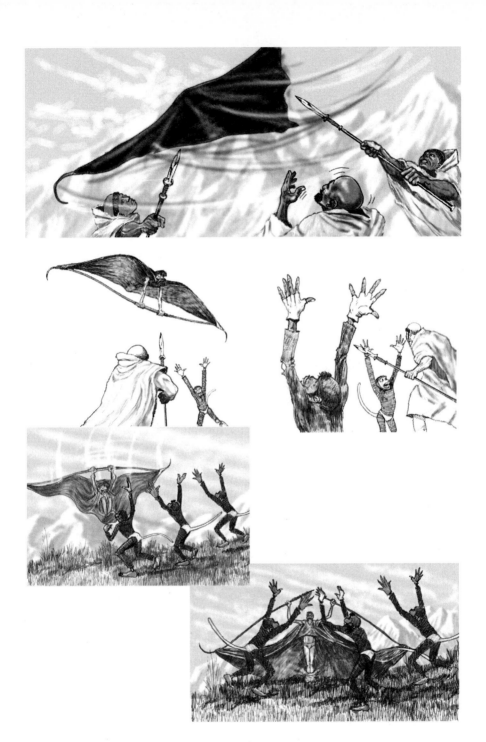

Teno frowned under his feather–fringed head–dress.
*I understand the seriousness of your situation.
Only people in extreme plight seek the council of
Chetemoto.*

Otasa stood to tower above the small bird man,
bending down to speak.
*At this very moment, my friend Teno, I fear that
this monster Venga is making his presence felt on
the Engelibizo plateau.*

Teno blinked as he assessed the information presented
to him.

He shook his head.
*This is most discomforting news. If you have been
able to reach our kingdom, then so can this Venga.
My King, Lipho, should hear of this without delay.*

He hooked the ends of the staffs into the wings, spread
them and connected them in the centre of a hide sleeve.
With effortless strides he was airborne and sped away
from the clearing towards the distant peaks.

Otasa realized, as Principal Don had quipped the Khuda
definitely could fly.

The Khuda.

Earlier in the history of the Mathiops a group of their species emerged with advanced agility and soon initiated experiments with various membranes, which enabled them to parachute from the mantle between the massive branches and onto the forest floor – they identified themselves as the Khuda. Between the Mathiops and the Khuda, a potential antinomy emerged. To prevent it developing into an antagonistic dichotomy the Khuda decided to move away from the forest to a place higher up the mountains where the giants trees did not impede their gliding skills, and, additionally, distant themselves from their gravity–bound cousins.

They settled on a skin cloaks manufactured from mountain goat hide, which possessed a remarkable tensility. They boiled the hide, cleaned and beat it into a thin, almost translucent sheet, before stitching them together to form the triangular shape of their wing design. Pockets and slings were added and a pair of staffs, tipped with bone talons, braced the cloak into a wing. The Khuda's light and lissome frames suspends easily beneath the large cloak. Deft at gliding across the deep valleys on the rising air currents, they could soar to the higher mountain plains and plateaus to hunt and forage for food and building material.

The mountain goat roamed the high plateaus and slopes in abundance, providing the Khuda with principle source of food and clothing. Using a

similar net to the Mathiops, the Khuda swooped in pairs to capture their prey. The taloned ends of the pikes doubled as weapons and hanging hooks, similar to bats.

With their aerobatic ability established, they could choose the most inaccessible terrain to build their communities. Huts – called nests – perched and braced off cliff faces, offering absolute security from all adversaries but the giant black condor. Like the Mathiops dwellings, they used ropes across the valley between the nests to create an infrastucture that could be used alternatively to the winged cloak. Steep ladders linking nests also lined the cliff faces.

Lipho, the current elected ruler of the Khuda mountain people, had watched over his people going about their daily affairs for four decades from his abode, which was the customary position of honour and positioned high on the cliff wall of the Valley–without–end..

Sitting cross–legged on a thick hide mat, with his long wisp of frail grey hair brushing across his craggy old face, he could survey the homes of the tiny mountain people, clinging to the opposite wall of the cliff face. They stretched in both directions far into the constant mist that swelled up from the huge cavity below.

Made of twine and poles with roofs of matted grass and leaves, covered in goat hide, the

construction methods had altered little from the Khuda's previous existence as part of the Mathiops. Lazy trails of smoke from cooking fires drifted up through the roofing material.

A diligent people, they moved about enjoying the freedom that their membrane wing offered. Old Lipho watched all the proceedings. Although his aging limbs denied him the thrills of flying, his mind remained active and he enjoyed the antics of his poeple and chuckled at the young novices practicing aerobatics, much of which they performed entirely for his benefit.

Lipho seldom spoke to his people. Their understanding of each other's roles in the society had been practiced for generations. The physical difficulties of their surroundings discouraged gatherings and ceremonies.

To compensate, as each of the mountain people set out for their daily tasks, they floated past the old leader's perch, looking in his direction to pay their respect. To see their old leader and receive a response with nod or a raised hand represented a bonus for the passing traffic. Lipho did his best to be present at the times when his people moved about the most.

Girls, selected for their beauty, cared for the old man, whom they regard as their collective grandfather. Once one of his maidens reached a marriageable age, suitors vied for her attention, performing humorous and dangerous maneouvres. Lipho decided who should be paired off for a life together – his decision always proved satisfactory.

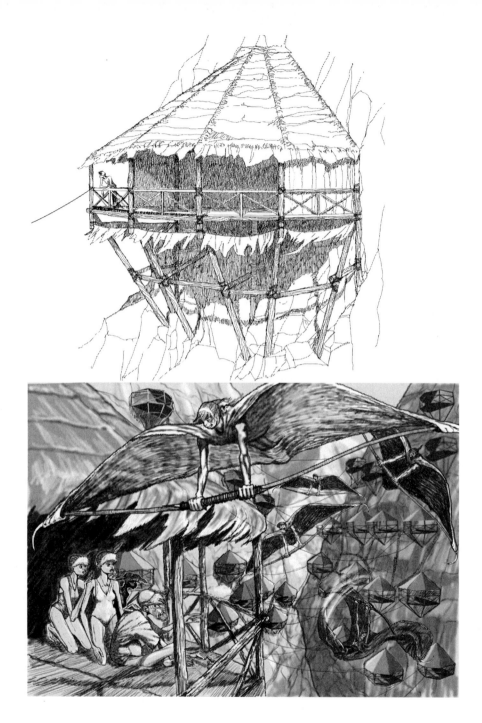

Then suddenly the Sabiluto turned a corner to enter the Valley–without–end and the Khuda settlement. From his vantage point Lipho saw the train of giants in green cloaks and their diminutive Mathiop escorts moving around the edge of the valley wall towards them.

Within moments Khuda flyers swarmed around the strangers. The expressions on the faces of Lipho's courtiers portrayed their anxiety at the appearance of the Sabiluto – the only respite being the accompanying Mathiops.

One veered from the activity and landed before Lipho. The man in front of Lipho folded back his cloak and announced,
They are from the plains, my liege. They come in peace – in search of Chetemoto.

Lipho frowned. Nothing had like this had happened before.
Why do they seek Chetemoto? They have never needed her council before.

The messenger explained in brief.
The Mathiops tell me that a demonic tyrant threatens the plains – a spirit being – a behemoth. They say the Hosiyosiku, the Queen of the Night, has recommended they approach Chetemoto.

189

Lipho saw his people guide the visitors to a plateau
further up the ravine, where they settled, exhausted.

Lipho commented to the messenger.
They must have been travelling for a long time to
reach us.

Indeed, your highness.

Lipho.
Make sure they are well treated and relay my greetings. We will assist in every way possible.

The man spread his cloak and coupled the staffs
together before falling into the valley space and
swooping up to the plateau.

The evening light glittered from the illuminated nests
that splattered the valley walls The plateau glowed with
several fires as the Khuda and their Mathiop cousins
attended to the Sabiluto and swapped information
– cachinnation mixed with the swirling rising mist.
While the Sabiluto recovered from their abrasions and
bruises, under the combined fussing of their guests and
guides, Otasa, positioned in full view near the edge of
the plateau, liaised with Lipho across the valley, using
several flyers to transfer and interpret messages.

Lipho's responses were always agreeable and bountiful
in praise for the Sabiluto's effort in reaching the Khuda
settlement – not an easy task

for such large people. He also explained that the Khuda, over the years, had experienced the occasional contact with Chetemoto.

They had seen her approaching along a certain route that led to a mystical place where steam erupted form the ground, mud bubbled up and fire spat from crevices – a dreaded sulphurous place. The Khuda never ventured into the realm of Chetemoto.

The Khuda's description of the high peaks from whence Chetemoto emerged had not been exaggerated. Otasa, not wishing to risk lives unnecessarily, took one guardsmen and one porter – both volunteered without hesitation.

The porter's physique equalled that of the guard – some would say more so. With Otasa between the guardsman in the lead and the powerful ever–vigilant porter in the rear, laden with two full shoulder–slung packs of provisions and blankets, they tentatively picked their way deep into the inhospitable terrain, encountering all of the features described.

After lacing through a forest that seemed to have foliage alive with enormous serpents and spiders they entered even a worse environment where molten mud and fire erupted around them and steam jets burst from the ground, sometimes almost beneath them The smell was unbearable, causing them to cough and clear their throats constantly.

Shaken, they eventually entered a clearing surrounded in a swirling wall of mist and steam. In the centre stood a staff the height of a man – it appeared cast from metal lava. It appeared to balance on its base, unsupported and hovering above the ground. An open torus surmounted its head with three spikes projecting in a trident from the sides and centre. An indistinct human figure shrouded in a black hooded cloak stood beyond it at the edge of the clearing, shimmering in the mist.

Otasa and the men stopped in front of the staff. Otasa raised his hand in greeting and called out in the steadiest voice he could muster.

He used the most confident voice he could muster.
Greetings. I am Otasa, Royal Councillor of the Sabiluto from the Engelibizo Plateau. I seek the council of one called Chetemoto.

The figure sauntered towards them and stood close in more distinction. It stopped behind the staff and looked at them through the torus. Its face hidden in the darkness of the hood with only snatches of the darting eyes discernible.

A wavering female voice replied.
I am Chetemoto, Commander of Fire. I have been expecting you. You have travelled far to seek my council – I shall not turn you away.

Otasa acknowledged the acceptance with a bow of his head. The figure circled around the staff and stood close to him; their faces aligned. He restrained a gag as the caught the malodorous stench emanating from the robe.

Then the robe fell to the ground to reveal an emaciated, putrescent and naked crone. Skin hung in damp folds, oozing mucus, pustules and festering sores everywhere. Her breasts were indistinguishable empty sacks. Yellow and bloodshot eyes blinked at him.

Through her putrid breath she uttered:
Place your hand upon my chest, Councillor Otasa. Touch my disease to confirm your commitment, or be gone.

Otasa reluctantly moved his open hand forward; his flesh looked so youthful by comparison. He swallowed to quell his rising nausea, but he could not suppress a shudder of repugnance. He felt her heat against his palm – hot, flame hot – like a fire. His skin was about to blister. He had to withdraw before it burnt. But with conviction shoved his hand forward again.

The hag burst into flame.

Otasa snatched back with a yell as the guard yanked him away, simultaneously thrusting his spear at the flaming apparition. Blisters burst in Otasa"a hand to reveal raw flesh; he gripped his

wrist in pain and sank to his knees. The guard flung his cloak around Otasa as protection. The porter had already dropped his packs and stood with clenched fists, ready for an attack.

But there, before them, the blazing apparition transformed into an amazing young woman. Only the startling Hosiyosiku could match her beauty. She had features more akin to the Sabiluto than the Baqala with high cheek bones and dark brown eyes.

Extended lashes that pulled up in the corners surrounded them. A delicate straight nose over full, perfect lips completed her visage. Her charcoal black hair was cropped short and covered in a web of beads that cascaded in a glistening blanket over her shoulders to her waist. Her light brown skin gleamed like polished ebony. She wore a beaded brassiere and loincloth, and fur slippers.

Otasa still on his knees bowed in homage, overcome. The guard and porter knelt supportively each side of him. So much had happened in recent times. From a stable and halcyon lifestyle, they had witnessed the manifestation of Venga, the desolation of the Engelibizo Plateau, the trek to the Mountains, the Vatope, the Mathiops, the Khuda, and now they had seen magic beyond their comprehension.

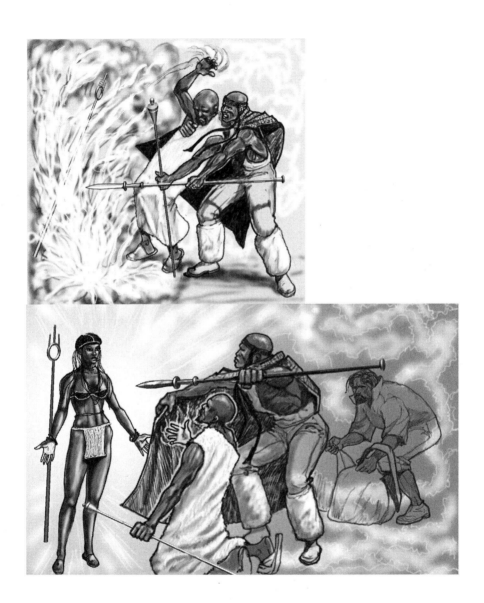

Chetemoto laughed at their response, and crouched directly in front of Otasa. She placed a warm soft hand on his forehead to comfort him.
Be calm, Otasa. There is much that needs to be explained. You must know all of these things if you are to overcome Venga. You must know the strength of his power and its limitations. Only then can I implement the Omen of Fire that has been cast for the Sabiluto.

She waived hand in a welcoming gesture.
Come, follow me – I"m sure you and your men would enjoy some refreshments.

She swung around and strode to the edge of the clearing. The staff floated next to her. Suspended in the strong arms of the guards, Otasa followed still clutching his smouldering hand.

Chetemoto spoke over her shoulder.
I'll get something for your hand.

They plunged through the churning wall of steam to emerge in a sun lit glade. It lay between a clear pool and forest of tall trees with only the vivid green lawn of the glade covering the ground between them.

A variety of brightly coloured birds flapped and chirped among the trees. Fish weaved through the clear water of the pool. At the far end a water fall trickled down th side of a low plateau. A more dense forest lay beyond the pool. Tranquillity immersed the whole scene.

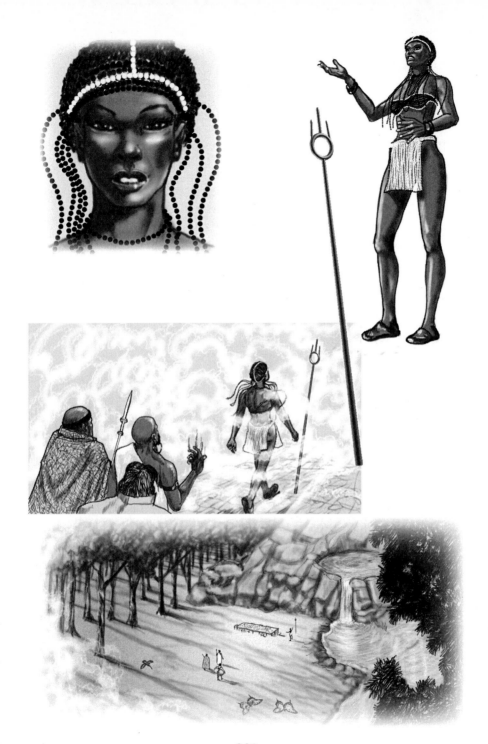

Chetemoto stood next a low table spread with fruit, beverages and meat. The staff followed her around – never out of reach. She beckoned the men so sit at the table.

She smile as she swept her hand over the offering.
Help yourself – there's plenty.

They did not hesitate.

She sat next to Otasa on the bench with her back to table and inspected his hand. She held her own hand open and a creamy ointment appeared. Gently she wiped the balm over his wounds. The flesh healed almost immediately.

While the men concentrated on their food, Chetemoto stood behind Otasa and placed her hands on his shoulders and leant towards him.
You must realize that it has been some time since I was in the presence of men such as yourselves. In fact, I would happily declare that I have never been in such a company of men. A councillor, forthright, brave, intelligent and committed.

She moved behind the Royal Guardsman, and again placed her hands on his broad shoulders.
A warrior; powerful, skilled at arms and equally devoted as his leader.

She gave him a squeeze of affection before turning to the porter. With her hands on his shoulders she announced.

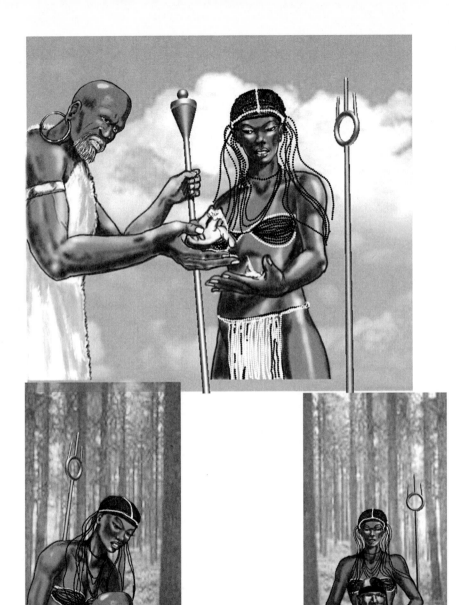

203

A Sabiliuto – stronger than any two men and who carries his physical and emotional burdens as if they were mere feathers.

She went around to the other end of table where she stood and looked at them in turn.
So, I will indulge this event for as long as practicable.

After consuming a pear, Chetemoto commenced with her discourse.
I need to explain how the spirits of the past re-emerged after so long in dormancy. The great upheaval of this continent threw everything back millennia into a time when the Spirit World dominated. Mtombo, The First of All Spirits, rose from the turbulence to empower selected mediums with commands.

There are three such commands – water, fire and wind. Mtombo retains the power of all three, which he can use to control the others. Water douses fire, yet fire can boil water and turn it to steam whereas wind can douse a fire or fan it into a rage and then water can quell a wind, especially dust storms, or between them create tumultuous typhoons. In turn Mtombo controls the bestowed mediums – or at least that was the plan.

This world is not perfect – not even the Spirit World.

She sniggered and selected another morsel. She munched and stood back to outstretch her arms; the staff hovered close to her open right hand.

In this region, I alone have been granted the command over fire. And only I can approach Mtombo to recommend another recipient. But the price is high for anyone chosen to seek such powers. I am loyal to Mtombo, as is Nyamanzi, Queen of the Engelibizo Waterways.

But Venga, with the command over wind has proved to be a poor choice by Mtombo and one he regrets, but he can do little to reverse the situation. Venga has grown too strong and even challenged Mtombo for the position as First of all Spirits. Fortunately, Mtombo inveigled Venga into a truce, whereupon he plunged him into the water of a deep river and entombed him.

Then an earthquake changed the course of the river, leaving Venga's prison isolated. It soon dried and Venga escaped with his power intact. Since then he has been roaming the continent subjugating beasts and humans in a tormented milieu – he has gone quite mad.

She looked at Otasa and extended a forefinger to emphasize her observation.

I presume you have encountered those fiendish acolytes of his – the vengazana.

Otasa looked blank, his mouth too full to reply. He did not know what she was talking about.

She walked around and stood beside Otasa.
His dust devils – they are called 'vengazana'. He creates them with his swatch. They are almost human in their cunning. Oh yes, be weary of his swatch.

She swished her hand in a demonstrative arc.
One flick from it blasts enough wind force to fling a large man through the air, usually to his death.

Otasa swallowed his food before responding.
Those dust devils – yes, we know all about them. What did you call them?

Vengazana.

He repeated.
Vengazana.

Chetemoto confirmed and nodded with an impish smile.
Yes, they are merciless. They swoop from nowhere onto unsuspecting humans and animals, and pulverize them in there crunching cones.

The consternation on her visitors' faces, prompted her to elaborate.

But they are powerless over water, or even damp ground, as they are unable to suck up the stones and dry grit they need to survive. And when the rains come, like their creator Venga, they disappear. Venga himself hibernates during the rainy season, so you will enjoy some respite from his tyranny.

Otasa and the two guards nodded with understanding.

Otasa added.
We have discovered this frailty for ourselves, and we have had some success over the vengazana dust devils.

Chetemoto sat backward on the bench and leant her elbows on the table.
Then you stand some chance of surviving Venga's predicted onslaught.

Otasa sensed that she did not wish to douse their slender grasp on hope.

Otasa crinkled his brow in thought.
You mentioned an Omen of Fire earlier. What is that?

Chetemoto tilted her head back and narrowed her eyes.

She clapped her hands together in a resolute gesture.

Rest and eat for now. Tonight I will seek the council
of Mtombo to find out the content of the omen
that he has prepared. As we have already heard
of Venga's ambitions for the Engelibizo Plateau
through the oracle Hosiyosiku and her necromancy
practices, perhaps we have been granted enough
time to consider counter actions.

The porter, almost disregarding her announcement,
removed his tunic to reveal his exceptional physique
and walked over to the pool where he plunged into the
cool refreshing water.

Otasa explained:
The Sabiluto ritually bathe everyday – sometimes
twice. The Baqala have a joke about that, we say
– all that water is why their hair grows long and
their skin is lighter than ours – it is because they've
washed out half the pigment – ha, ha, ha.

Chetemoto rose and walked away with a smirk.

She pointed to a pile of blankets.
Your bedding,

And, without another word, was soon out of sight
among the trees.

In the pool the porter pondered his thoughts:
*Ah, but I suspect it will be the power of
water; not fire, that will eventually save
the Sabiluto – for it was beneath water
that Venga was originally entombed."*

Wrapped in their blankets the men slept soundly under a balmy starlit night.

Chetemoto's voice awoke them as she approached with her loyal staff in accompaniment.
Good morning everybody – I trust you all slept well.

A chorus of **morning** between yawns answered her greeting.

She stood authoritatively in front of them with her left hand on her hip as they disentangled themselves from the bedding. The staff took up a commanding position in front of her. She ran the forefinger of her right hand around the inside of the torus that supported the tridents.

The men noticed that the table and its victuals had gone.

She spoke to them while looking through the torus.
Mtombo imparted to me that a saviour will be presented to the Sabiluto. This saviour will be delivered in fire from the sky as a child. He will have white skin like ash and hair like flames. As he will be born of fire, so we will call him ZALOMLILO – the one born of fire, or ZALO for short.

She stepped aside the staff and splayed her hands,
briefly closing her eyes.

Some time will elapse before Zalo arrives –
whereupon, he must be brought to me under
complete secrecy the moment he is delivered.
If Venga learns of his existence, he will stop at
nothing to destroy the infant.

She placed a hand on her chest.
As I am aware of the prediction, so Venga will have
learned of it. His vigilance will be relentless.

Chetemoto turned around with her arms spread.
But here, safe from the reach of Venga's power, I
will edify Zalo through the arduous process that
Mtombo demands for candidates to qualify for a
command – this will take years. As I alone will be
Zalo's mentor, his command will be of fire through a
staff like mine.

She prodded the staff with an elegant forefinger,
rocking it back.
In the mean time, not being short of humour,
Mtombo will send a spirit being in the form of a
teenage Sabiluto girl who is totally duplicitous;
Sizana will be her name.

Not only will she be inconceivably arrogant.

Chetemoto chuckled and waved a nonchalant gesture.

As well being beautiful, her intellect will be breathtaking. She will do everything possible that appears to bolster Venga's plans, yet at the same time keep Mtombo informed.

She smiled knowingly.

I can only assume that the plan will be to give Venga enough rope to hang himself.

She folded her arms across her chest in a submissive expression.

But Venga will be powerless to stop her, or even harm her.

She laughed at the proposition.

Ha, Ha, I think he is going to be so infuriated at this girl's presence, he will go quite peculiar – ha, ha, ha.

She gripped the staff and pointed it forward. A hazy cloud formed before them.

This is an image of Sizana.

Then from its midst a form emerged – a holograph. She stood with her back braced in an arrogant arch and her knuckles on her hips. Her chin lifted as she looked at them with aloof detachment. She could only be described as beautiful.

Her bountiful shoulder–length hair had a slight tinge of red that turned the black slightly brown. Her skin was more pale than most Sabiluto and, although she wore a Sabiluto skirt and leggings, the distinct breast plate of white beads and a black diagonal cross distinguished her as a member of Venga's court.

Chetemoto noticed the broad grin of approval from the porter.
Ah, I see, the porter is impressed.

He replied:
Wow – I think I'm in love.

Chetemoto displayed annoyance at the porter's flippancy. She vaporizes the image and the cloud with a **poof** sound from the staff.
Well, she hasn't been created for the likes of you, Sabiluto porter.

She emphasized **porter** with a distinct frown of disapproval to remind him of his status.

She continued and stretched her arms wide as she looked to the sky and released the staff. The staff hovered above her, holding its torus in line with her face as though it was a magnifying glass.
Here, safe from the reach of Venga's power, I will edify Zalo through the arduous process that Mtombo demands to qualify for a command: this will take years. As I alone will be Zalo's mentor, his command will be of fire through a staff like mine. It will be known as the staff of fire – Dondomlilo.

The porter continued with his apathy and paid little attention to her proclamation as he packed away their paraphernalia while humming to himself. Otasa and the guard are astonished at his disinterest.

Annoyed, Chetemoto snatched up the staff and demolished a large tree with a roaring jet of fire–balls. Otasa and the guard stepped back in surprise. The guard swept his cloak across them as protection from the blast.

Chetemoto attempting to gain the porters attention, flung her arms forward expressively.
This is the kind of power that Zalo will have with dondomlilo. No living thing can resist the heat; it will incinerate every human, creature and vegetation in its path. The vengazana will vaporize into glass crystals, the Bavenga soldiers will burn into ash – their weapons will melt into pig iron.

223

Without hesitation she aimed the staff at the rock face at the end of the glade and blasted boulders into molten lava while announcing:

Blast rock into liquid.

Then she plunged the staff into the pool, which erupted into boiling steam.

Boil water in an instant.

She returned to a more passive posture and extended a forefinger. The staff resumed it customary position next to her

She inhaled to calm her voice.

But first there must be Zalo. As I said before, nothing is perfect in this world – so let's see how it all turns out.

The porter picked up a half eaten chicken leg left from the previous days meal and chuckled.

Mmm, I guess you didn't need any help cooking the meat then.

Chetemoto's temper flared at the porter's lack of dismay at her performance.

You are not very impressed, Sabiluto porter. Your attitude is highly provocative. Maybe after this episode you will change your mind, porter.

With defiance the porter took a step towards her – his voice emphatic.

My mind, perhaps yes – my belief never.

Perturbed at the interaction Otasa intervened. His nervousness expressed in a film of perspiration.

He waved a hand vigorously with alarm.

Please, great oracle, he is not a believer, Chetemoto – none of the Sabiluto believe in the spirit world. Not like the Baqala – we hold your powers in awe.

Chetemoto scowled at the defiant porter with narrowed eyes..

For your sake, porter, I hope that you have good reason for this attitude. Sabiluto – it means 'fear nothing'. But I could incinerate you where you stand. Do you not fear me?

The porter shook his head slowly.

Incinerating me would deem you no better than Venga. You would have lost your cause before it has even begun. What would have me fear more – incineration from you or pulverisation from Venga?

Their eyes stayed locked for a moment before Chetemoto turned her head and waved a dismissive hand.

Hmph – well, you've heard the omen – now begone.

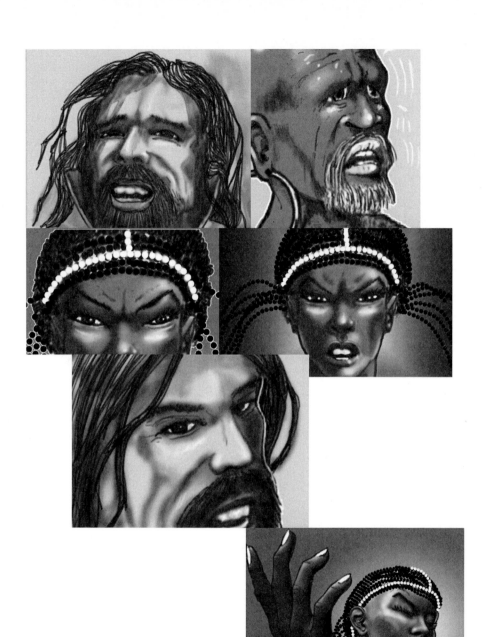

Indignant, she erupted in a ball of fire, emits an eerie cackle and shot away in a fiery shroud with the staff propelling it forward.

The men watch the spectacle vanish into the woodlands.

After a brief pause, Otasa turned to the porter.
You seem extremely confident in the presence of such a powerful oracle, porter. You have a reason to be so?

The porter completed packing the sling bags and looped each one around his head so they hung each side of him. He looked up at Otasa and the guard both awaiting his response.

He announced with assertion.
I am a Master Maker, as was my father – that was before one of Venga's stampeding herds trampled him into gore in an isolated field.

The other men stared at him, taken aback.

Otasa flicked his hand towards the porter.
A Master Maker – you mean you belong to the Secret Society of Master Makers.

The porter adjusted his load for comfort and stepped towards the clod bank through which they had come the day before.
Yes, that I do, Councillor Otasa. Yes, that I most definitely do belong to the Secret Society of Master Makers – my name is Enzayo.

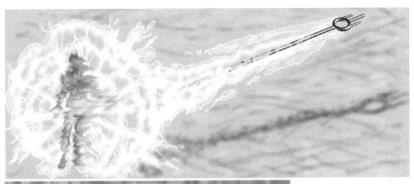

The Secret Society of Master Makers (the SOMM).

.The wide Chimvura River flowed from the Swamplands in the North, through the Engelibizo Plateau to plunge in an array of spectacular waterfalls down the escarpment into a vast ocean delta. The Chimvura segmented one quarter of the plateau against the eastern range of rugged terrain, where The Master Makers lived and worked in their construction camps isolated from the greater plateau during the four–month wet season when the Chimvura reached its turbulent capacity.

The eastern side of the river was the original entry point to the plateau for the Sabiluto centuries before a group of them decided to remain on that side of the river, as a haven, should there be a problem for the others who ventured forward. They were responsible for constructing rafts for the venturers to cross the river.

In their absence, the river subsided allowing them to erect a pontoon bridge. Soon after, they introduced several ferry services to link them to the plateau. As their collective skills distinguished them from the main group so they decided to emphasize their position and form and exclusive society.

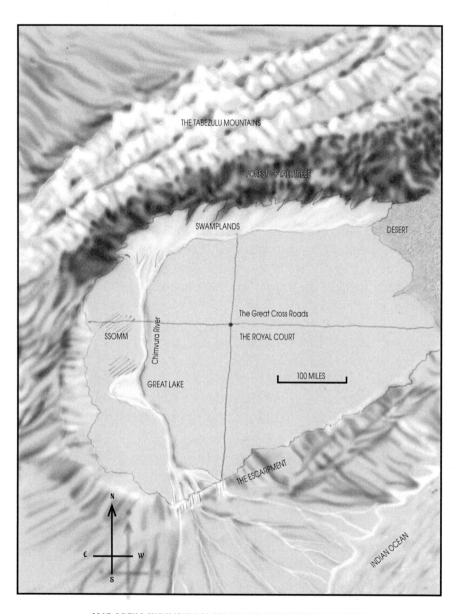

MAP OF THE ENGELIBIZO PLATEAU AND SURROUNDING FEATURES

Sworn to secrecy and living and working by strict codes, they established the Master Makers. Using primary technology, such as billow furnaces, foundry techniques with iron and steel alloys, they constructed windmill components, weapons and tools for the Royal Guard and Villagers, including supervision of building operations and clay brick and tile manufacturing.

They planned and implement the vast irrigation network and numerous wells that covered the fertile plateau and provided the clay pipes tot supply fresh water and flush away sewerage. Saws and axes for the forestry undertakings were one of their more demanded products.

Being this self-sufficient, and relying on their nepotistic conventions, the Master Makers did not abide the spiritual beliefs that the Baqala and some Sabiluto pursued. They were committed to solving all problems through the rational and pragmatic activity of science.

They were dedicated to a focused and healthy morality along with intense physical development, which they required to manhandle and transport their assorted and hefty products.

Over time, the plethora of myths surrounding the Master Makers had elevated their status into legend – no one ever questioned or rebuked their presence or efforts.

Ingalane Camp

The arrival of the Chetemoto searches, returning from the mountains to the Ingalane camp, was ambivalent. The searchers, although overjoyed to be back from the mountains carrying their invigorating experience with Chetemoto and her prophecy, a major concern had arisen since their departure – no news had been received from Potonoka. He and his party seemed to have vanished.

Although much work had been accomplished at Ingalane in the construction of dwellings and utility buildings, the Sabiluto told him that even greater achievements had taken place below. Overlooking the tops of the forest trees, Otasa could see the smoke from the settlement below drifting upward with a reminiscent redolence of a traditional Sabiluto village.

He breathed in deeply to suppress his emotions – Engelibizo seemed so far away. Interjecting his thoughts was the final gesture that Chetemoto had made – a demonic cackle that reverberated through his mind, stimulating doubts about their future and her intentions.

The access through the fissure had been modified to include step and all the loose rocks had been removed. In addition, grip ropes and nets lined the walls at awkward points.

As they emerged from the fissure and into the forest jubilation bounded around them. Tela, Gono, the other Sabilutos, Principal Don, his wife, Edna, and a swarm of Mathiops greeted them with beaming enthusiasm. The news that they had found Chetemoto had preceded them.

Otasa shook his head in disbelief at the development of the settlement under Tela's vigorous encouragement. Tiers of covered platforms linked between trees and random stone paths crossed the dank forest floor.

Three stone ovens and chimneys sat on a podium and a wood-curing shed was already half-filled with cut logs. A jumble of excited explanations accompanied each part of the structures as they were to Otasa.

The Mathiops pole and rope construction methodology captivated everyone – Enzayo in particular. The three floor levels of frames were prepared on the ground and lifted into position with handrails holding them in place. The handrails were later extended into a pole and rope lattice that wraps around the exterior of the structure.

Another quirky method was the use of bamboo halves that were lapped into one another and laid at a slope to create a roof covering. To hold the roof together a continuous rope was looped around supporting purlins and fed between the

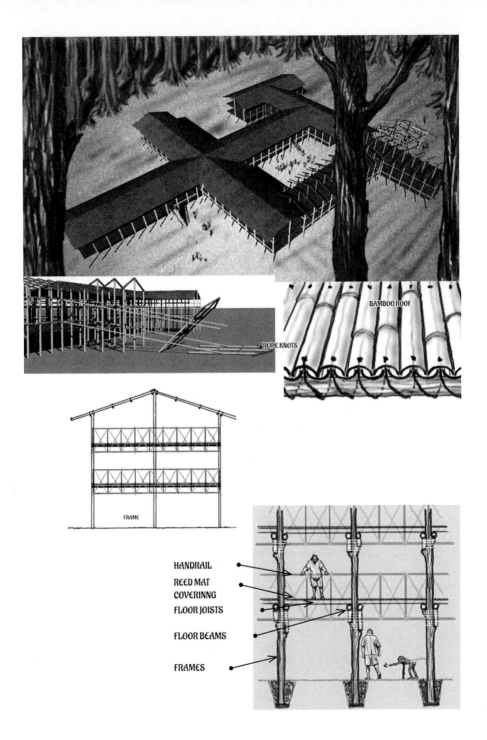

BAMBOO ROOF

ROPE KNOTS

FRAME

HANDRAIL

REED MAT
COVERINNG

FLOOR JOISTS

FLOOR BEAMS

FRAMES

valley bamboos then through a hole in the ridging
bamboo; a knot was tied and the rope fed back through
the hole and around the purlin again, pulling the ridge
bamboo down into the valleys and against the purlin –
a glob of gum water seals the knot hole.

Don and Edna could not emit words fast enough,
explaining how they had combined their knowledge
of pole construction with the Sabiluto's wood and stone
working tools – tools that the Mathiops knew about but
had never thought them necessary until now.

They marvelled at how easily the Sabiluto adzes had
been able to split the thick bamboo stalks, hollow them
out to cup in each other to form the durable waterproof
roofs; a process that the Mathiops had achieved but
with exceptional difficulty. They were also intrigued at
how the Sabiluto bolsters had split rock and how they
had built kilns and stoves for cooking meat – now that
was a new experience for the Mathiops. They vowed
they would never eat raw meat again and laughed at
their callowness.

The babbling embraced Otasa as Tela led him to a flight
of stairs that climbed to a central platform with skins
covering the floor where Tela introduced Otasa to his
quarters. He was seated on a rudimentary bench from
which he could overlook the growing settlement. But
despite his overwhelming admiration for their effort, he
could not disregard his anxiety for his brother.

239

As soon as the opportunity arose, Otasa instructed Tela to arrange a search party. The Mathiops provided a support group to traverse the canopy along the route Potonoka had taken, while the Sabiluto scouts covered the ground. The Mathiops had made an earlier attempt to find Potonoka, but avoided venturing to close to the forest floor, for fear of encountering the cannibal Taals.

At the first opportunity, The Master Maker Enzayo drew Tela and Gono aside to inform him of his deliberations over the meeting with Chetemoto.

He beckoned them to secluded place where he assessed no one is listening – even from the surrounding foliage. In any case Enzayo lived in an environment of secrecy, so he continued within the comfort of that condition.

He told them quietly.
Tela, by all accounts, you are the one who is most likely to be elected as the Talisman of future events, so it is in you that I will confide.

Firstly, my name is Enzayo, Master Maker. I volunteered as a porter in order to find out all that I could about the nature of the aberrancy that befalls us, so that I could prepare the Sabiluto for the advent of Venga.

Enzayo moved further into the seclusion of the undergrowth, to where Tala and Gona followed.

At the outset, it must be understood that the debacle in which we find ourselves is purely the doing of the Spirit World – their inter feuding and arrogance has bought about Venga's surge in power and advance into the human domain.

They alone are responsible for the destruction of so much of our existence and so many of our families and they will have to make recompenses – I do not regard them in any position other than culpable. Their power displays do not distinguish their responsibility – they are guilty.

Enzayo clinched his fist emphatically.

Several facts are obvious to me. The people of the Spirit World are powerless to directly intervene in Venga's activity as he is one of them.

That being so they have to have some human intermediaries to transmit their intentions, hence the choice of this Zalo, whoever he turns out to be. And Venga needs a human army to enforce his edicts – without them, he is diminished.

He paused to gather his thoughts.

In addition, all the spirit beings need some sort of device to deliver their powers. For example

243

Chetemoto has a staff and she told us that Venga uses a fly swish to create his vengazana and other wind forces.

Enzayo bumped his fists together.
But I need more advanced technology.

Enzayo emphasized his next point with a waving forefinger.
All of these factors give me the confidence that, as a Master Maker I will, along with any other Master Makers, we can construct weapons of war to fight the Bavenga army.

It was me, while working on the water towers at the Royal Court, who hastily prepared the water jets that repelled the vengazana – I can do better – I will do better.

But Tela shook his head..
Where can you get that technology Enzayo. We only nurtured the technology we needed – there are no other sources – you are our technology resource.

Again Enzayo raised a forefinger.
The Mathiops, Tela – the Mathiops hold the key. I heard that Lady Edna has a recall that extends for two thousand years. Somewhere in there, she has to know facts that I can interpret into weapons and devices.

You must convince councillor Otasa to persuade the Mathiops to divulge their knowledge – even though they detest the influence and degradation that technological abuse brings. The Mathiops are the key to our success whereas Zalo is the key to spirit world's success. But make the promise to the Mathiops, Tela, that every bit – every particle of the technology used – will be destroyed when Venga has been ousted.

Tela held his hands to his lips in contemplation.

Leave it to me, Enzayo – i'll see what I can do.

Four days later Mathiops raced through the canopy
to Potonoka, breathless they yelled.
  We've found the remains of a guardsman – it's
  terrible – he appears to have been eaten alive.

In unison the Mathiops on the ground retorted.
  The TAALS.

Soon after another group of Mathiops swung into
the camp, their message:
  We've found them – they're captive in Taal village.

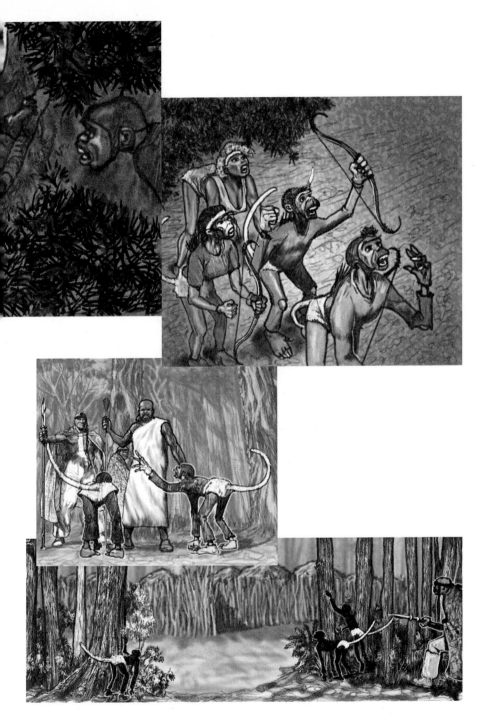

The Taals.

They could best be described as having a pale
complexion and a squat muscular figures that were
high waisted with bulbous midriffs and long arms.
A large head with long matted hair completed their
appearance.

Heavy angry brows festooned small darting black
eyes, thick noses and thick red pouting lips presented
a saturnine mien – yet they could break into a dazzling
smile, exhibiting strong white regular teeth, albeit with
the incisors filed to points.

Resulting form another botched experiment, the Taals
were reincarnated from extinct Neanderthal DNA
to resolve the conundrum of human longevity. The
Technos believed that the key lay with this species,
convinced that it was during their period the life span of
the human diminished dramatically.

Some scientist suggested that the earlier Neanderthal
could have lived for two hundred years or more, and
only through interbreeding did the life span reduce to
slightly more than thirty years.

The Technos claimed that they had been able to isolate
the DNA from an original species, from which they could
build a new specimen to be used for experimentation and
the development of implants

that could prolong human life indefinitely without infection.

That efficacy did not materialized, leaving the scientists with a tribe of perverted cannibals who turned on themselves for sustenance and licentious gratification. The scenes in the laboratory compound that housed them defied the most gruesome hallucinations, Heironymus Bosch's image of Hell was tame by comparison.

Unable to bear the decadence any longer, and having already deposited the Mathiops in the remote forestation of Nova Afrika, the Technos undertook a similar operation. But the Taals acclimatized rapidly and developed numerous villages. Their strength and ability with their throwing axes proved devastating on the fauna, including the Mathiops who moved to places out of reach.

Once the boar and deer also moved away from the convenience of the Taals, they reverted to their innate habit and struck at each other, with cannibalistic resolve, depleting their numbers dramatically.

Concealed in a thicket a short distance from the Taal village, the Sabiluto gather to formulate a plan of attack. Principal Don explained what the Mathiops have discovered. Using an arrow, he drew a rough layout of the Taal village in the dirt.

253

He explained:

> From the trees, we can see where the men are
> held – here in this hut next the fence.

He drew more circles in the dirt.

> All the huts lie against the fence. I think they fear
> fire the most because their huts are made of grass
> and leaves, so there is an open area in the centre
> where they gather and cook their meals – it's the
> only safe place for a fire.

> We estimate about forty Taals live in the village.

A guardsman who had returned from a reconnoitre
of the Taal village contributed to the scenario.

> The fence is too thick and the entrance too narrow
> for a direct assault.

Otasa had to ask:

> What about my brother – did you see my brother?

Principal Don and Edna stood Close together with
forlorn expressions. Principal Don prodded his arrow
into a circle that represented a hut close to the fence
and uttered solemnly.

> We did not see your brother, but we did see the
> Taals take a Sabiluto from that hut and execute
> him. They then proceed to cut him up to cook him.
> We believe the other men are being kept alive in that
> hut – sort of like in a human larder.

They remained silent for some time staring at the diagram on the ground and the arrow jabbed into one.

Principal Don unlooped his bow from his shoulders, pulled back the string and aimed down an imaginary arrow.
From the surrounding trees, we could fire arrows into their camp...

Otasa suddenly lit with inspiration with a demonstrative forefinger thrusting the air.
Yes, but even better – burning arrows.

Principal Don looked up at the councillor with a grin.
Ah, ha – I believe we have the birth of a plan, Councillor Otasa.

Otasa grinned back in confirmation.

Expeditiously, Otasa assembled his group in a concealed thicket out of view from the Taals' camp where he reviewed the circumstances.

A high fence of sturdy tree trunks protected the Taal camp. The entrance comprised of a curved narrow tunnel, which only allowed for a single file of men to negotiate in a crouch and easy prey at any point – attacking that way would be futile.

Otasa knew that only surprise and decisive action would accomplish a successful attack. Urgency dispensed any elaboration as each day that passed another proud

warrior would be consumed. The one assumption that kept them encouraged was that the Taals had not killed all the warriors. They were being kept alive for as long as possible as live flesh did not decay.

Otasa sat propped against a tree trunk deep in thought. He drew with stick in the sand in front of him. A short distance away the Principal Don sat crouched, holding his bow, and starred at the councillor. The two sat this way for a while then the Don stood up, and walked over to fire where a quick meal had been prepared.

He rummaged in the undergrowth next to the fire, and pulled out some dry grass. He wrapped it around the end of one of his arrows, binding it with a thin tread of bark. He placed the end in the fire. It started to burn.

He positioned the arrow in his bow and turned to face Otasa. He pointed the arrow in the direction of the councillor and fired it into some grass at his side. The grass started to smoulder then burst into flame.

Otasa jumped to his feet and stamped out the fire before it spread any further. All the men in the camp looked at him. He walked over to the apeman, placed a hand on each shoulder and grinned.
Yes, Principal Don, now we definitely have a plan.

After working frantically through the night, at dawn the next day, groups of Sabiluto and guardsmen gather to attack. Heavy pointed staffs were stacked in readiness near the village fence.

Another group worked quietly and vigorously to break through the fence adjacent to the hut where their comrades were being held. Otasa stood behind his men holding his ebony staff.

The low light defined the golden earring that looped Otasa's shoulder. Although tired – they had not slept – tension peaked their prowess. Their preparations demanded every second of every minute. They could sleep tomorrow.

Behind Otasa stood the Mathiops with their bows. Each Sabiluto held a straight, sharpened and heavy wooden staff with more piled beside them. They laid their metal bladed spears on the ground in front of them in readiness.

All eyes focused on the dark mass of trees that protruded into the night sky beyond the cannibals" enclosure. Don, next to Otasa, barely reaching waist height, stood, like the others in silence, waiting.

Everything depended on the Mathiop archers concealed in the trees. Their task deemed crucial and difficult to achieve. It had taken since dusk for them to indicate their readiness. Now it verged on happening.

To Otasa's right, the Sabiluto still worked silently
and frantically against the enclosure wall. They
dug quietly at a point opposite to the hut which the
Mathiops had established represented the larder
containing the Sabiluto captives and soon dragged
away part of the matted thorn shrubs that protected
the bottom of the wall They then loosening and eased
away the trunks and branches of the fortification.
One of them stood up and faced Otasa and he raized
thumb – they were through.

Otasa held his staff high and towards the canopy of
trees behind the village where the Mathiops hid in
readiness and he waved the staff back and forth – it
was time.

Like a tiny firefly, they saw a small light arc through
the darkness and fall into the enclosure – a burning
arrow fired from the Mathiops vantage point indicated
acknowledgement – the attack had begun.

Another burning arrow followed then three more fell
simultaneously, then five, a wave of them followed,
falling in a sparkling shower. They waited. An anxious
murmur of anxiety swept through the men unable to see
the events behind the fence fortification.

Otasa checked them.
Wait.

Slowly, resembling a huge billowing apparition, a cloud of smoke swelled upwards above the enclosure. Ripples of crackling flames reflected under it. The guardsmen readied themselves, raising their staffs into throwing positions. The Mathiops slipped arrows from quivers and placed them across their bows. The moment approached rapidly.

A surge of flames leapt skyward. They heard a scream from inside the camp, then shouting. The incrementing flames burst higher, lighting the area.

To escape their burning huts, the Taals had to run into the open centre of their camp. The Mathiops in the trees above could see them clearly in the firelight and fired at them

Otasa once again controlled his tense warriors.
Wait.

Again, a single lighted arrow arched high into the sky and fell towards them – the signal. Most of the huts were alight with the Taals huddled in the central clearing, making sporadic attempts to douse the fires. But the conical roof coverings of dried leaves and vines vigorously succumbed to the flames, there was little the Taals could do.

Outside, Otasa's men poised to launch their staffs. They had rigorously practised the trajectory and distance.

Otasa swung his staff with all his might.
Now

The warriors hurled their staffs into the sky and over the wall. Otasa heard the swish as the Mathiops released a fusillade of arrows behind them. The archers in the tree picked their targets accurately. The staffs and arrows rained down through the smoke, skewering the startled Taals through feet, through heads and arched backs – escape was futile.

The needle sharp staffs plunged right through bodies into those huddled below. The arrows fell in a black cloud until they covered the ground of the camp, resembling a layer of stiff grass. Some of the victims ran back into burning huts to be consumed as the burning roofs collapsed.

Some Taals scrambled for the narrow entrance, but a single Guard blocks their escape. With his sweeping cloak he deflected their blows from their axes and clubs and rhythmically plunged his word into their bodies until the entrance lay deep in dying and writhing Taals.

Mathiops outside the fence scrambled up to the top where they contributed to the onslaught of arrows into the huddled foe. Others leapt to the ground where they could deliver more accurate shots.

Tela and Gono climbed the fence to perch above the entrance where the gaurdsman had filled the entrance. Several Taals who had escaped with minor injuries rushed towards the entrance. They clambered over the corpses to attack the guardsman but with steady and accurate shots from their powerful bows Tela and Gono thwarted their attempt and shot them all.

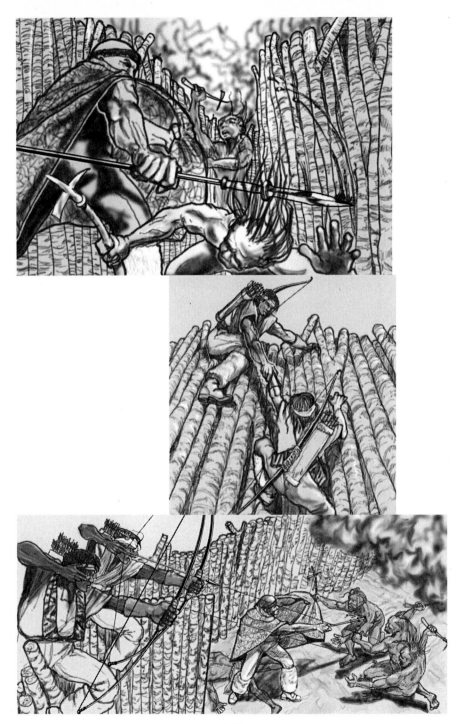

A man ran up to Otasa,

He panted excitedly.
We have got through to the hut, my master.

Otasa turned to the men still throwing their lances over the fence.

He yelled and raced to the opening in the fence where he thrust his staff at the opening.
Sabiluto – follow me – men of the Royal Guard avenge your comrades – spare no one.

A wave of green cloaks and flashing swords plunged through the fence opening. The first warriors hacked his way into the prison hut – the stench of decaying flesh and excrement momentarily stunned him.

In the flickering light through the door the Sabiluto could see victims stripped and lain crammed together, each spread-eagled on their back with spikes skewering their wrists and ankles to the floor.

Several guardsmen tumbled through the opening into the hut, just as a Taal appeared at the doorway gripping an axe. Before he could react the well–honed blade of a Sabiluto spear split his skull.

Two guardsmen moved their half-dead companions aside to form a path as the attackers streamed through the opening and into the burning camp.

With savage determination they screamed and charged at the Taal now dazed and confused in the forest of lances and arrows. Most of them were injured and the rest were dead.

Some were skewered to the ground while others attempted to jerk lances and arrows from their limbs, torsos and feet. They groaned and yelped with the pain and anguish.

With slashing blades from the guards" swords, either in hand or still on their staffs, the Sabiluto dispensed their assault efficiently and without compassion. The few Taals who remained uninjured to offer a token resistance were disposed of in swift decisive actions.

The wounded were executed where they lay. Some Taals attempted to climb the outer wall but were terminated in swarms of Mathips arrows –

there were no survivors. The ground of the central area squelched into a gory mud that splatterd the Sabiluto up to their knees.

Otasa entered the larder hut and attended to the captives. Of the forty who made up the original group, only twenty-two remained. Most of their hands and feet had rotted away from the spikes, leaving them near to death from starvation.

Still and silent against the back wall lay Potonoka. Carefully Otasa drew the spikes from his limbs. The councillor smiled weakly as his eyes gradually focused on his brother who now cradled his head in his arms.

Otasa comforted him.
Do not speak, my faithful brother. You are safe now – you are safe now.

They carried the survivors from the hut to view the vengeance that had been dealt to their captors.

Potonoka croaked weakly.
Are there any alive?

Otasa declared.
None, my brother – not one. Their seed has ended.

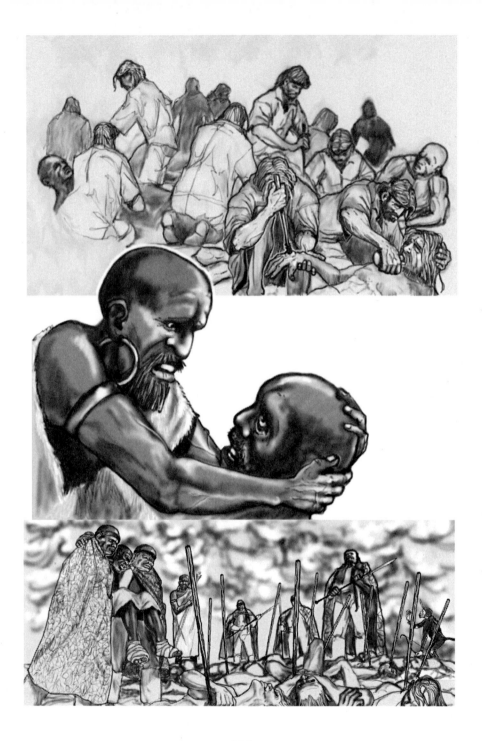

Principal Don plodded across the wobbly carpet
of corpses towards the councillors. He stood before
Potonoka and handed him back his golden earring,
which the Taals had ripped from his ear lobe.

Principal Don informed Otasa,
One of the Taals, presumably their leader, had been
wearing it as a necklace.

Potonoka blinked through his dazed condition at
Principal Don – he thought that he had surely gone mad
– a monkey had just spoken to his brother.

The other Sabiluto who had been rescued were totally
bemused at their first encounter with the Mathiops. But
as the understanding filtered through their cognizance
that they were among their saviours, jubilant
expressions abounded.

Despite the malevolence of the cannibalistic Taals, for
the Mathiops and the Sabiluto, this was the first time
they had killed members of the human species – sadly it
would not be the last.

With extreme care, the Sabiluto transported their injured
surviving comrades back to the forest settlement.
Principal Don and Edna suggested that the settlement
be called Potonoka in laudation of the suffering endured
at the hands of the Taals.

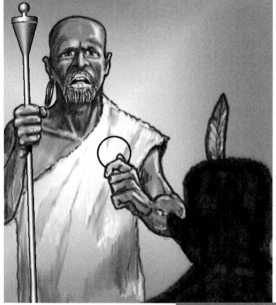

En route, Potonoka related how the Taals managed to subjugate them.

They were so exited at our arrival near their village. Their chief was extremely affable and instructed the young women to lavish us with food and fresh water. He said they had special honey–water that they collected each day from the dew of a honey–flavoured tree that they cultivated – it was a lie. The water had been drugged.

They young women acted flirtatiously and seemed in awe at our physical appearance. We had not been in the company of women for some time – we had little resistance to their advances. In a few moments, one by one, we fell unconscious.

We awoke where you found us. They kept us doped with their honey–water. They were well versed in their craft and knew exactly how to keep us fresh for as long as they needed.

It was clear that some of the victims would loose hands and feet as the infection had advanced beyond curing; others, more fortunate, would loose some functions in their extremities but nothing else – no one would escape any disability.

The Potonoka settlement soon established a routine with many Mathiops opting to integrate with the Sabiluto, especially as carers for the disabled men. They showed a genuine desire to be wanted and performed their voluntary task with cheerful enthusiasm.

The chatter and banter of the Potonoka settlement resonated constantly among the giant and majestic forest trees. A Mathiop maiden, noticing Potonoka's torn–away ear lobe, fashioned a silk loop to hang around his ear from which dangled the councillor's gold ear–ring

But the time for serious decisions had arrived as they had to return to the Engelibizo Plateau to spread the messages of the omen that Chetemoto had delivered. Obviously the disabled men could not return and they would remain.

Others who would be in extreme jeopardy if they were to return, in particular Otasa and the Royal Guardsmen, also remained at the settlement. The Sabiluto who had volunteered as porters would be the best to infiltrate without much attention, as would Tela and Gono.

 Not only were they to spread the prophecy that Chetemoto had declared about a saviour called Zalo, someone had to be there to locate and bring the child to the Potonoka settlement for onward delivery to Chetemoto. The onus of this task fell to Tela and Gono.

Enzayo declared that he would prefer to return to The Somm and prepare whatever he could to defend the Sabiluto, or at least make

the Bavenga presence as uncomfortable as he possibly could. It was in this regard that Lady Edna agreed to divulge as much as she could remember about the weapons of the past.

Unfortunately, much of her knowledge was literal with little visual, practical or scientific data to support it. Nevertheless, there were some aspects that Enzayo extracted with delight in the knowledge that he could provide and construct all the necessary components – gun powder and ballistics headed the list, closely followed by the theories of hydraulics and pneumatics.

Aeronautics fascinated Enzayo, having witnessed the capabilities of the flying Khuda mountain people, but it did not offer any tangible contribution at that time. The idea of a hot air balloon attracted more interest. It all seemed so simple when it was revealed that he did admit feeling humbled at the inability of the Master Makers to realize these facts for themselves.

One thing that did make him feel intellectually inferior lay in the principle of the propeller. For centuries the Master Makers had constructed windmills, without appreciating that the same device that operated the mechanism – the propeller – could also drive an object through air and, in a reverse action, through water.

Some Guards and Villagers decided that they would return to various areas of the plateau disguised as roaming soothsayers, to spread the word of the omen and the coming of the saviour. It would be dangerous work, as they did not know the intensity of Venga's proposed vigilance, yet it was obvious from what they had already experienced that there would be little room for error.

The rest of the Sabiluto would prepare and fortify the Potonoka settlement as the clandestine sanctuary against Venga's hegemony. The Mathiops and the Vatope agreed to participate and ensure that the route through the swamps and approaches were constantly patrolled for any indication of suspect travellers.

It was understood that many Sabiluto would want to travel to the settlement, but these numbers had to be controlled so as not to reveal the camps locate. The Vatope took on the task of conducting the screening.

Once the system had been established Enzayo, Tela and Gono returned to their respective home villages were they found Venga already ensconced.

The Reign of Venga

The Bavenga army, after disembarking from their vast fleet that transported them from Venga's former depleted empire, ascend the escarpment to the Engelibizo Plateau. In tens of thousands, they flood the Great West road as they marched inland in serried rows.

Perhaps it was the collective knowledge of the Omen of Fire and the impending arrival of Zalo that imbued a condition of acquiescence in the Sabiluto nation as the Bavenga streamed over the escarpment and onto the Engelibizo Plateau. They commandeered whatever they chose as accommodation, supplies and services with the fiendish Vengazana in constant accompaniment.

The Royal Guard first saw the flood of the approaching army bearing down on the Royal Court along the Southern Cross Road that led from the escarpment above the coastal plains. They encircled the Place of the Throne in a human tsunami and then flowed down the other Great Roads and into the heart of the kingdom.

The guards and Sabiluto Hunters undertook a brave attempt to protect the Royal Court and its occupants, but the number of Bavenga overwhelmed them in a brutal surge. The Bavenga encircled the Royal Court and vanquished the surrounding settlements in a sweeping torch of fire and destruction.

King Thaba, the Councillors, the Royal Guard and
their families were isolated in a swamp of Bavenga.
There was little attempt at confrontation, no threats or
challenges so the Bavenga merely sealed them off in
their terraced domain.

And all around the fiendish Vengazana whirlwinds
swirled under the glowering stare of the gargantuan
phantom of Venga on the horizon; monitoring events
and pulverising suspected dissidents indiscriminately.

The Bavenga raided every village, except the Baqala,
and remove all able–bodied adults, male and female
with the orders that the construction of a stone citadel
was to be built on the site of the Royal Village forthwith.

The remaining guardsmen, King Taba, his family,
Councillors and all the court attendants were
unceremoniously herded into a stockade to await their
destiny in putrescent conditions. The Sabiluto knew that
further resistance was a romantic aspiration and would
prove futile against Venga's inimitable powers and the
thousands of Bavenga soldiers pervaded their land.

A few who, having lost all their families and friends in
the initial onslaught, chose dissent and drifted into the
wilderness in small bands to live as

vagrant opportunist raiders. But their existence only aggravated the vigilance with which the Bavenga and the Vengazanas operated. Soon the invaders had secured the entire plateau and the monitoring behemoth cloud that hovered permanently on the horizon established its significance as the effigy of authority.

As one Sabiluto observed,
Why couldn't Venga simply have a flag.

One exception to the domination resisted – the Somm. The Vengazana could not cross the Chimvura River as all attempts from the Bavenga army were decimated under a hail of projectiles launched from a bank of mobile trebuchets across the wide water.

The Bavenga learned to leave the The Somm alone but maintained a constant vigilance along the river and developed a wall of fortifications. Sporadically, patrols would be suddenly smashed under a load of missiles from The Somm. The guard duty along the Chimvura River evolved into a punishment posting.

Venga's ascension to power had no fanfare or defining moment such as that of a coronation or victory parade, it merely imparted its existence through the actions and orders of the Bavenga who were fierce, ruthless soldiers and dedicated to their master.

The Bavenga comprised of mercenaries carefully selected for their physical and fighting prowess even comparable to the finest of the Royal Guard. Their attire distinguished their identity and comprised of broad black–hide bands that crossed over the chest and a large white animal–hair head–dress with three black stripes sweeping from a metal head band hung across the width of their shoulders.

Heavily armed with a variety swords knives, spears, they also used a sharp–edged bull whip as a favoured means of administering their authority – one lash could sever flesh to the bone, even amputate an arm or hand of more frail individuals.

They employed the weapon unconscionably taking delight in the extent of the injury and mutation a single slash could achieve with children and pretty girls – choice targets. The Bavenga issued a tenet that Venga could only be referred to as MambomuVenga, the Ruler of Hate, or the MushemuMepo, the Master of the Wind.

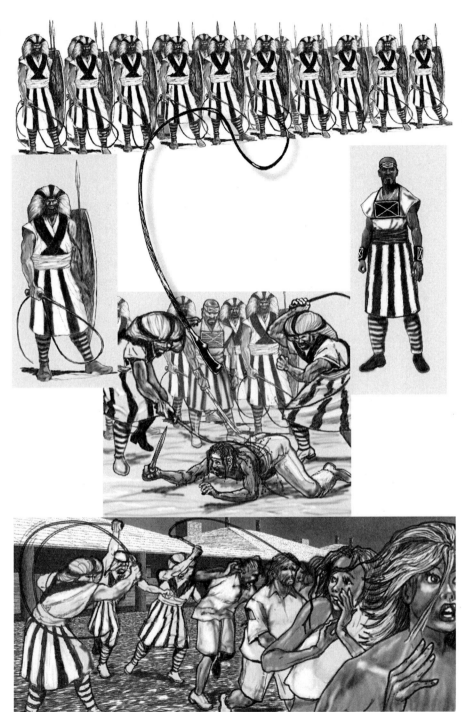

MambomuVenga's exigent priority was to construct a vast citadel of stone on the site of the battered Royal Village, compelling the Sabiluto to enlarge their skills of quarrying and masonry, hitherto a tertiary undertaking, as they preferred clay brick as basic construction component.

As the Bavenga permeated through the Sabiluto nation they enacted another Venga edict – in each village a teenage girl, usually between twelve and fifteen, with the highest intellect was selected to undergo training in ciphering under the tutelage of Soothsayers and Runners. As village Scribe the objective of the girls was to record on a scroll the lineage of each member of her village for three generations.

The scroll once complete to current conditions, had to be displayed prominently in the central communal shelter, and updated as the circumstances dictated. In addition, the Scribes had to learn the technique of tattooing from the Baqala, as the canon demanded that each Sabiluto had to have their names inscribed indelibly and legibly on their left deltoid.

The tattoo had to be in white and done so that the letters, once the incision had healed, raised above the skin in an embossing. The left shoulder had to be left exposed at all times to facilitate instant identification, which manifested yet another unique idiosyncrasy of the Sabiluto

The Baqala played a significant role in the exercise, not only providing their tattooing skills to ensure the embossing occurred, but also in the supply of the permanent titanium dye and selected white thorns, specially treated and honed as applicators. They prepared soporific pacifiers for infants and local anesthetics to apply on the areas of the skin before the operation began.

The Bavenga placed an exigency on the operation – any person not so marked at the end of that rainy season would be executed. The Scribes worked fervidly without rest to ensure that they were not responsible for the death of one of their village. At the conclusion of the undertaking, the young Scribes collapsed exhausted.

As only the presence of water disrupted the vengazanas and it was the only effective defence the Sabiluto had against them. Damp earth or grass swiftly reduced the dust devils to useless mounds of mud, and they could not traverse any stretch of water, not even a puddle in the road. So when the rains arrived, the Sabiluto breath a sigh of relief at the few months of reprieve from the tyrannical whirlwinds. Also, the quarries ceased to operate.

The huge fires extinguished and the slippery sides and sudden storms rendering the supervision of the workers too dangerous for the Bavenga, offering another brief respite It also compelled Venga and his followers hibernate into a cycle of debauchery

and gluttony. The subjugated Sabiluto had no option but to fulfil all the Bavenga's demands until the plains once again dry out.

As rain and fire were believed to be in the sole control of the First of all Spirits, Mtombo, the exhausted Sabiluto learned to regard Mtombo as their only spiritual ally and waited patiently for the arrival of Zalo.

Any resistance or acts of bravado were dealt with fatal resolve, which directed the demoralized and defenceless villagers to work in the quarries, located in the East where large round and bulbous stone hills filled the terrain. There the Sabiluto shatter the rock layers into blocks, using fire and water.

Even the once shielded Sabiluto women were humiliated into the building operation. They were required to sort, select and stack the heavy stone blocks into their various sizes. Their hands and bodies were soon etched in scars from handling the uncompromising stones with jaggered and sharp edges.

Many perish before they manage to develop the necessary survival skills. The heavily armed Bavenga effected their orders under they constant flaying of their sharp–edged bull whips, taking sadistic glee in their punishments.

The stone blocks were transported to the Place of the Throne on rudimentary sleighs. The Place of the Throne had been renamed

The Citadel. Under the direction of Bavenga captains the huge outer wall begins to rize outside the perimeter wall of the settlement. Within weeks the area has been enclosed, preventing any escape or delivery of supplies.

Most involved in the construction of the citadel had little appreciation of the enormity of the undertaking, until the outer walls began to climb in a methodical and shallow batter form the edge of the surrounding trench. Venga's builders supervised the positioning of each stone block, laid dry without mortar yet bonded with amazing accuracy.

Only the black granite, peeled in layers from bulbous volcanic features, was selected for use. The natural layers of the granite hills determined the dimensionality of the blocks, as the stone masons lit huge fires to heat the rock surfaces and then swiftly doused them with water – the resulting contraction would shatter the surface layer and separate it form the one underneath.

The masons then cut the fragments into manageable blocks. The incessant wood smoke, blasts of exploding rock and the clanging of mallets on steel bolsters congested the ambiance of the Engelibizo Plateau.

As the Citadel wall rose it became evident that

the inhabitants of the King's palace were to be entombed – Venga was merely going to build over the top of them, there to slowly die in a windowless and airless tomb.

But as soon as the Citadel wall reached the level of the first terrace, one member of the Royal Court manages to escape and surrender to the Bavenga; and offer his services – Bakati, the Royal Diviner.

He fell to his knees in subjugated humility before the fist Bavenga captain he could find.
O mighty captain, I beseech you to listen – I am Bakati, the Royal Diviner. All Baqala and Sabiluto do my bidding. I am their spiritual mentor.

Without my persuasion they will demonstrate unnecessary resistance and make your task that much more difficult. I will coerce them into servitude. And to your great leader, I devote my allegiance.

On the northern point of the outer wall a tower was the first of the superstructures erected. Once complete the phantom giant cloud on the horizon raced across the plains and blasted into the tower – the roar could be heard across the plateau – Venga had arrived in person.

The Vengazanas

As MushemuMepo, the Master of the Wind, named Venga created his Vengazanas with his fly switch. He whipped the thongs around while pointing them to the floor to start a small whirlwind, which grew in intensity as he chanted and danced around, encouraging it with vilifications, and within moments a vigorous whirlwind surrounded him.

Once a Vengazana spun vigorously, Venga delivered his instructions and dispatched it on its mission. On its departure it soon developed into a minor cyclone.

From the edge of the citadel's perimeter wall, the conical tower rose as the pre–eminent structure. Once complete, a solitary figure appeared on its apex platform – Venga. For the first time the Sabiluto saw their oppressor in a natural form, albeit too far for absolute recognition. But on the tower Venga began creating his Vengazanas and the true purpose of its existence became evident.

The quantity and size of the new Vengazanas outstripped anything they had witnessed previously. The Vengazanas omitted a shrill screech before speeding down the tower to the ground where they sucked up stones and debris to increment their volume and sculpt their vague fluttering human features to resemble angry eyes and snarling mouths.

These new Vengazanas possessed one positive
objective – to administer Venga's punishments, usually
executions. The size and intensity of the Vengazanas"
motion could pulverize a human in seconds, far more
effectively than before. There was no escape them.

They displayed the ability to seek out a quarry
anywhere. Once latched onto a victim with their
meandering tail, they could snatch them into their
interior where the maelstrom of stone, rocks and other
material acted like a crusher, ripping limbs from torsos
and flesh from bones, and all the while resonating their
shrill screech of glee. On completion of their demonic
retribution they disgorge the remains scattering them for
the numerous carrion to consume.

As was well known the presence of water disrupted
the Vengazanas and it remained the only effective
defence against them. Damp earth or grass swiftly
reduced the dust devils to useless mounds of mud and
they could not traverse any stretch of water – not even
a puddle in the road.

Concealing bladders of water in various accessible
locations had saved the life of many unsuspecting
victim on more than one occasion, but the retribution
for destroying a Vengazana was ultimate if discovered.
Learning from this tactic Venga often sent his swirling
assassins in pairs or groups to efficate his instructions.

When the rains arrived, the Sabiluto breathed a sigh of relief at the few months of reprieve from the tyrannical whirlwinds. During this period the Bavenga army stimulated their activities in an attempt to bridge the shortfall. Although it did not entirely compensate, it did offer some slender solace from the constant oppression.

The Hunters were compelled to cull the vast herds of antelope and buffalo to provide the Bavenga camps with a constant and plentiful supply of freshly cooked meat – their favourite food. With despair the Hunters performed their bloody task in the knowledge that the carnage was not sustainable.

Also, during the wet season, the stone quarries ceased to operate. The slippery sides and sudden floods proved too dangerous for the Bavenga to supervize the workers, offering another brief respite. Venga and his followers hibernate until the plains dry out.

The Sabiluto constructed a sprawling settlement for the Bavenga that surrounded the Citadel in a protective cocoon. Through the network of narrow streets and always the Sabiluto toiled in servitude, providing domestic chores and gargantuan meals for the gluttonous hefty soldiers.

The acquiescent Sabiluto women attend to the ruthless men who ravage them without compassion, often sublimating them with concoctions of narcotics. The women consumed the potions in copious quantities in the hope that it would either kill them or permanently erase their memories.

The Sabiluto had reached the nadir of their identity. Rain and hope remained the only respite too their subjugated existence. The only real resistance came from across the great Chimvura River where the SOMM maintained an isolated stronghold, For Venga they were more of a nuisance than an threat. The river was as much their defence as it was their captor.

Every heart of the Sabiluto prayed in silence for the coming of their saviour Zalo – but for many the fantasy of the omen had become a mere myth.

The pride of the Sabiluto nation had been sequestrated.

Next - Commander of Fire